A Bucket List Birthday

Emmie J Holland

Contents

For anyone who has ever felt their existence was a burden.
You are not a burden. You are human.

Trigger Warnings

Dear Reader,

It is my desire to ensure that everyone who picks up this book feels comfortable in doing so. Because of this, I have provided a list of trigger warnings. Be kind to yourselves

Explicit Sexual Scenes

Swearing

Mentions of Loss

Mentions of Cancer

Challenging Family Relationships

One

Ellis

My grandfather had a stroke during my fifth birthday party.

I mean, he was fine.

He still is.

In fact, he currently lives in upstate New York with my grandmother and spends nearly all of his retirement hunting and trying out new recipes.

I would be lying if I didn't admit that watching my family sob while my grandfather got carried off on a stretcher didn't spark a new core memory. And this memory was certainly painted blue.

I would also be lying if I said I didn't think about it every year around my birthday. It's like the ghost of birthdays' past decided I had cute shoes, then followed me around for the rest of my natural life, thinking we were destined to become best friends.

We were not.

Destined to become friends, that is.

The pencil scratching across paper draws me back to the present. The sounds of coffee grinding and gentle murmurs remind me I'm in full control of the ghost. It's only allowed to haunt me when I say it can, despite what my approaching birthday says.

I pause, looking at the composition of lines and shadow on the page–the way the values build into something recognizable–something *good*.

My eyes flick up to the old couple sitting by the window of the coffee shop, sipping espresso and smiling in a way that says they've lived a long, full life together. I can't help the way the corner of my mouth turns up at the image, and I glance down at my sketchbook again. I'd like to think I did them justice.

"I hope you told that sweet couple you were doing that first. I'd hate for my best friend to be thrown into prison for stalking strangers."

I slam the sketchbook shut, finding Lennon hovering above my table of choice with a coffee in her hand. She smiles, her freckles bunching, before she slides into the seat across from me.

"I didn't ask them," I admit as she takes off her coat and drapes it over the back of the chair, leaving the heathered gray beanie on her head.

"Pity," Lennon muses, one eyebrow cocked. "I won't visit you in prison, you know. Our friendship will cease to exist. I simply hate talking on the phone, and that would be the only way we could communicate." She takes a sip of her coffee before picking up each braid to analyze the split ends of her red hair. Finally, her blue eyes meet mine. "I simply can't do it. It gives me anxiety."

I chuckle, tapping the pencil on the pine surface of the table. "I'll think of you often, while I'm gone."

Her smile cracks wide, a true testament to my best friend's actual heart—the one she hides beneath hurled insults and sarcasm. "I would hope."

Lennon and I met in college and trauma bonded over having the worst roommates in the history of all roommates ever. I would argue that my roommate was, objectively, worse than the girl inhabiting Lennon's dorm room. She would argue the opposite.

Now, some six years later, we still live in the same city and spend most of our time hanging out. You know what they say about trauma bonding.

Well, I'm not actually sure what they say, but regardless, we are still friends. And I still invited her for coffee after work.

"So," she begins, pulling her legs up onto the chair. "I heard something important is happening in six days."

I roll my eyes. "Yeah?" I question, knowing full well where this conversation is headed.

"Oh yeah. Winter solstice. It's a very important day for fantasy readers." She rolls her tongue along her cheek, trying to suppress her amused expression, but it doesn't work. Her shining blue eyes give her away. "For witches, too."

"Thank you for the reminder," I say, trying to keep the fabricated look of annoyance plastered to my face. "I nearly forgot to add dancing naked in the winter forest to my planner."

Lennon huffs out a laugh before leaning down to grab a small box from her backpack. "No, but really," she starts. The red bow decorating the gift wrapped in black paper reveals the truth. Despite her quips, Lennon cares.

Tapping the outside of the package once, she slides it across the table toward me. "Happy early birthday, Ellie."

I grab the box, carefully pulling at the ribbon and slowly peeling back a corner of the paper. "I'd say you shouldn't have, but considering the fact that you leave tonight for Minneapolis, and you won't be back until after my birthday–"

"Yeah, yeah," she says, waving a hand. "I owe you for missing your twenty-fifth birthday. It's not like you're eighty-two, dude. We still have time."

I halt my assault on the gift, deadpanning. "I could die at any moment," I say. "A piano could fall from the sky as soon as we leave this coffee shop."

Lennon places her elbows on the table and cocks her head to the side. "Ha," she says. "Considering the fact that you're describing every cartoon ever, I'm sure you'll live. You'll just be flattened like a pancake."

I snort a laugh before responding. "At least we'll have matching chests, then."

Her chuckle floats across the table, and I'm reminded of all the reasons I stick around Lennon. For starters, she's the most honest person I know, and something about that makes her feel incredibly safe. It gives my anxious brain the freedom to be honest, too–to let go and not think so hard about everything I do and say and how it is going to affect the people around me.

She loves jokes–especially when they're bitchy.

Bitchy is Lennon's favorite pastime.

"I'm taking the gift back," she remarks, but I know she doesn't mean it.

As I rip the paper open, the last scrap falls away before I turn the package over to read what's inside.

Charcoal pencils for drawing.

My chest warms, and I look up to find Lennon's satisfied expression. She glances once at the sketchbook still resting on the table's surface. "Have fun in prison," she says. "Sorry, I'm poor. I'll bring something else back from The Mall of America. I know they're just art pencils."

"You know I don't care," I say, tucking a black strand of hair behind my ear. "Besides, these are the expensive ones, anyway."

"High price, high quality," she states before taking a sip of her coffee.

"Sometimes." The smile dances on my lips before I watch the couple sitting across the way stand up to leave. I consider, just briefly, giving them the drawing, but then think better of it. While Lennon's suggestion of prison is just slightly on the side of *too far*, I am certain a disgusted look and an awkward "*how nice,*" are completely on the table. I would like to avoid both.

"So, how's the dungeon?" she asks.

My gaze draws away from the couple and back to Lennon. *The Dungeon* happens to be the name of my new office location. For some insane reason, the company decided that during the building renovations, they would move the marketing team to the basement. Maybe it's because they believe we are chronically online. I suppose social media is part of the job, but I don't understand why I have to sit in a frigid, leaking office space with exposed piping that reminds me of a horror movie.

The lights flicker and everything.

"I'm hoping they mean it this time when they say three more weeks," I offer. Leaning forward for emphasis, I cradle my lukewarm coffee carefully in an attempt to keep it from spilling. "I don't understand why they didn't just move everyone in accounting down there. Anyone who gets off on Excel spreadsheets filled with numbers and data would probably love being cut off from civilization."

"Still not getting to the coffee machine in the morning?"

I let out a breath, throwing my hands in the air. "It's like five miles away, and you know how I am about appearing late!"

"You wouldn't be late, Ellis. You're literally still in the building."

My nose scrunches in disgust. For someone who has known me for six years, Lennon really doesn't understand me at all. "I refuse to *appear* late, and I also refuse to wake up earlier than seven."

She snorts. "No sense. Not even a little."

My phone buzzes on the table, and I pick it up, reading the text message from my aunt.

Beatrice: *Eloise is practically buzzing with excitement. Can't wait to see you!*

"Shit." My heart drops so fast, I'm afraid it might fall right out of my asshole. When I look at the time, I realize that I have exactly seventeen minutes to drive twenty minutes away from the coffee shop. "I totally forgot I had to watch Eloise tonight."

"B has a hot date?"

I stand up, shoving my sketchbook into my backpack on the floor before pulling my coat on. "With her husband, yes." I wince. "I happen to be the babysitter tonight."

"You're the babysitter every night." Lennon taps a finger on the table, her eyes sparkling with challenge. There's a subtle dig beneath her words, written in the tone and her expression, but I'm not ready to acknowledge it.

She isn't wrong, but she isn't right either. It's not like I have some crazy job or boyfriend that requires all my attention. I can help Beatrice out every once in a while. It's the least I can do.

Aunt B found herself fresh out of college with a thirteen-year-old child after my mother passed. And while she never made me feel like a burden, there were challenges. She met her husband, Brian, at thirty. The entire thing had been a long time coming. B didn't date before Brian—not after me, that is. Just another blue memory, I suppose.

Long story short—Beatrice sacrificed her twenties, and the least I can do is watch Eloise a few Fridays a month.

"I'm sorry," I say, throwing a pleading look at Lennon and pulling the bag over my shoulder. "I promise I'll make it up to you when you get back from Minneapolis."

She sighs, standing up and drawing me into a warm embrace. "You better," she says, her tone turning teasing. "I didn't buy those pencils for nothing."

I chuckle, grabbing my half-empty coffee cup and bringing it with me as I rush out the door. The bells bang against the glass as I exit, cold biting as soon as I'm out in the fresh air.

The wind swirls around the sidewalk, a reminder that winter is coming, and all the other warnings thrown onto memes from the internet. Since it hasn't snowed yet this year, the trees remain barren and the gray sky casts gloom all over the city street, covering the world in sorrow. It's the perfect time for seasonal depression.

Combine that with my residence in the dungeon and lack of vitamin D—all kinds, really—and I'm one minor inconvenience from a Zoloft prescription and an empty bank account due to all the therapy I need.

I fumble with my car keys, stabbing them into the lock because the key fob stopped working months ago, and I'm too lazy to get it fixed. If the weather doesn't transform from stick season to winter wonderland soon, my therapy bill will be the next excuse.

I curse when the keys slip from my hand and land on the ground. Placing my coffee on the top of the car, I bend over to grab them, only to be met with the cup sliding from the surface of my Chevy and smacking me in the head.

It's like middle school gym class all over again.

I curse, feeling the now lukewarm coffee seep through my coat and into the back of my shirt.

"You're actually kidding," I mutter, feeling the wet strands of hair at the base of my neck. I look at the empty coffee cup on the ground and consider leaving it for dead. Then I remember Lennon refused to visit me in prison and pick it up to avoid littering.

That's when I hear a soft chuckle behind me. I spin, my eyes locking with the stranger getting into his car one spot over.

Tall, dark hair, slim build, handsome. Did I mention tall? I look up and up to see the ghost of a smile on the stranger's face–proof that he was the one to make the sound.

My face twists into something entirely unpleasant. "Did you just laugh at me?" I question.

The man's smile drops as he pulls the door of his car open. "Absolutely not," he says, brows furrowed.

I watch as his hazel eyes meet mine once more before he climbs into the car, starts the engine, and pulls away without another glance.

"Rude," I mutter before crawling into the front seat and shoving my useless coffee cup into my designated trash bag.

I start the car, careful to keep my back off the seat in the hopes that I won't be reminded of the fact that I just got hit in the head with coffee. And if that isn't embarrassing enough, a handsome stranger just happened to be lurking in the parking lot in time to both watch my coffee disaster and laugh at me for it.

Definitely just like middle school gym class.

I glance at the clock on the dash and realize I have ten minutes to get to Aunt B's.

"Shit," I whisper, putting the car into drive and pulling away.

Two

Ellis

"B, I'm so sorry I'm late."

I shouted my apology into the dimly lit entryway after plowing through the front door. I quickly peel my coat off and grab a hanger from the closet, holding it up and noticing the dark stain on the back collar.

I thought buying a beige coat would save me from the coffee spills, but apparently, there was no escape from the coffee stains. It's like the entire world needs to know you're an addict.

After shoving the coat into the neatly organized closet, I pause to feel the back of my gray T-shirt, noting that it's almost dry. I wipe the minimal amount of dampness on my high-waisted jeans, realizing I look like a mess.

"It's alright." B's heels click on the wooden stairs as she descends toward the front door. Her fingers fumble with her earring. She's wearing a short black dress, her shoulder-length hair pinned back with dark strands escaping around her face–the only sign of her true state of distress.

Those wispy hairs remind me of the twenty-four-year-old B raising a thirteen-year-old Ellis. Those first few years were a mess of dirty kitchen sinks, not nearly enough space, and the kind of hopeless fumbling that brought us closer together. Over time, B seemed to organize her life, her scattered thoughts, and somehow buried her hopes and dreams along with it. She'd lost her sister, and along with it, her carefree spirit.

And then she met Brian.

Her voice doesn't betray its usual calm. Everything about B seems cool and collected, except for those wispy strands of hair–the ones framing her sharp features and letting me know how rushed she really is.

The guilt instantly swirls in my gut.

While she's been nothing but kind to me, I know that getting off schedule bothers her. Whether or not she admits to it is a different story.

Small footsteps skitter down the long hallway leading into the kitchen, and Eloise lunges herself into my arms with Brian trailing behind her, adjusting the sleeves of his suit jacket.

Whatever date they had planned, it's *nice*.

That churning of guilt becomes a wild storm as I realize they must have a reservation, and here I am, conveniently forgetting my responsibilities and showing up fifteen minutes late.

"Ellie, you have to see my new trampoline." Eloise smiles brightly from where she stands in front of me, her bronze skin glowing as she glances at Brian. "Can I show her, Daddy?"

"A trampoline?" I question, standing up to my full height and watching B move to the closet to grab her own coat. She pauses for a moment before pulling the garment off the hanger and shrugging it on. Her pale hand brushes the stray baby hairs away from her face as if she's trying to smooth out her distress.

"It's not what you think," B says, starting at the buttons on the long peacoat. "Just one of those little exercise trampolines someone was getting rid of at the office. It's currently decorating the center of our living room."

Brian's deep chuckle sounds through the entryway as he presses a kiss to his wife's temple before wrapping Eloise into a warm hug. He stands up, turning to look at B, his full lips pressed into a firm line. When he speaks, I can tell he's treading lightly. "Did you tell her?" he asks.

"Tell me what?" I'm looking between my aunt and her husband, listening to the sounds of Eloise's little footsteps retreat down the hallway.

B huffs and rolls her eyes. "Brian's parents bought us a little Christmas gift." She finishes buttoning the top button on her coat, her brown eyes meeting mine. There's an apology there, and I start to question what she could possibly have to say.

Brian cuts in before she can explain, rubbing a hand on the back of his neck nervously—hall light illuminating his dark skin with a gentle glow. "It's not exactly little," he corrects. "They bought us a cruise package."

Confusion wraps around me as I look between them. "Oh, that's great!" I say. And I mean it. A smile plays on my lips as I try to puzzle out why this seems to be bad news.

B sighs. "Yeah, well. We leave in two days."

"Oh." My smile falls, disappointment blending with the guilt to make an interesting cocktail in my stomach. "How long will—"

"I'm so sorry," B says, dragging me in for a hug. She smells like oranges and spice, and I let the familiar scent envelop me. There's a warmth to her hug, a reminder that while my mother's death made her orderly and punctual, it never once made her cold. "They didn't tell us, and I didn't want to miss your birthday this year, but I figured Lennon could keep you company, anyway."

I clear my throat. "Right." I refuse to admit that Lennon is leaving too—meaning I will spend my birthday with Netflix and maybe a good bottle of wine. It's not that I want to lie to B, I just don't want her to worry about me. The woman has been worrying since the age of twenty-four. She's put me first in a lot of ways, and now I'm finally watching her live the life she'd dreamed of.

I watched B sacrifice a lot for me growing up. The idea that I'm the same age that she was when I came to live with her still shocks me. B is determined and put everything on hold for me–her career, her love life–all of it had to wait until she figured everything out.

It was a heavy load to carry.

Not to mention the fact that my father was nowhere to be seen. I never knew him–had never met him, and the death of my mother didn't change anything. He never came around.

It used to bother me, but I've since let go. It's much easier that way.

"No worries!" I say as Eloise comes rushing to the door again. "I had plans, anyway." Eloise's little hand grabs mine, and she drags me down the hall to the kitchen, leaving her parents in the dust. "You guys will have fun!" I call out.

I hear B's gentle *thanks* just as I'm accosted by the four-year-old trying to rip my arm out of its socket. For a tiny thing, she's pretty strong.

I rub my shoulder when she crosses the kitchen to dig into the cabinet. "Mommy bought popcorn for our movie night," she squeals and begins foraging in the large bin at the bottom of the pantry used for snacks. Once she finds what she's looking for, she bolts upright, holding out the box.

"Movie theater butter," I say, grabbing the popcorn from her hands. "My favorite. What movie were you thinking, little Ellie?"

"Anything but monsters," Eloise declares, her face falling into a serious expression–like she's about to tell me national secrets and expects me to listen with the utmost interest and discretion. "I had a story behind my eyes last night about those, and when I tried to get into Mommy and Daddy's room, the door was just locked!" She huffs, stomping a foot on the ground. "They took a lot of time opening it, and I know they were awake. I could hear them playing around before I knocked. I don't know what they were doing, but it must have been very fun." Her face scrunches briefly before she exclaims, "And loud!"

A laugh escapes my lips as I slip my finger beneath the cardboard to open the box. I hold on to more laughter as I place the bag in the microwave.

So, maybe her earlier expression was correct. She certainly revealed secrets that B would consider *highly sensitive*. Not that Eloise knows that. "No monsters," I say. "I also want to see that new trampoline of yours."

• • • ● • ● • • •

I'm on my third popsicle when I really start feeling sorry for myself.

The lights are off in the house. The soft sound of white noise drifts from upstairs as I watch another video from some reptile rescue in California. I should stop, though.

One of the geckos didn't make it, and I shed at least four tears for the tiny guy. I guess I'm just in my feels–or maybe I'm just a lizard person. Not the conspiracy kind. More like the equivalent of a dog person, but for lizards. Who knows?

Lennon texted me to remind me how much she loves me, and that she can't wait to stop by my house when she gets back from her trip, and that somehow made me feel worse–not better.

The popsicle drips onto the front of my shirt, and I look down at the red stain at my stomach. I didn't mean to tie-dye the thing with food and drink today, but I guess we don't always get what we want.

Like quality time on our birthdays.

What a stupid love language to have, anyway.

The clock ticks in the kitchen, and I decide I'm done with the popsicle. It's not like I haven't had two others already, and I'm a grown-ass woman. It's time to start acting like it.

Getting up, I go to the kitchen where I toss the thing in the trash can and pull out my phone after feeling it buzz in my pocket.

Lennon: *I'm sorry you'll be alone on your birthday, boo. You should throw yourself the biggest party, or better yet, hire an event planner to do it for you.*

I chuckle, tapping the marble counter before typing out my response.

Me: *Yes, I'll just hire someone to plan me a day. It'll be the very peak of my entire existence. Not sad at all.*

I look at the text, lingering for a moment before pressing send.

While I meant it to be a joke, the seed of a thought grows in my mind. Technically speaking, I could just hire someone to plan a day for me. Maybe there's a sad freelancer who wouldn't mind putting together a solo birthday bash before Christmas.

I roll my tongue against my cheek, staring at my phone and questioning my sanity.

It would be pitiful.

It would be absolutely ridiculous.

It would prove that I'm a friendless oaf in desperate need of a life–or possibly a few dozen cats. Or lizards.

It would be rock bottom, and I wouldn't even have a divorce or a need to file bankruptcy to show for it.

The clock continues ticking, and I finally open up a web page.

I drag the name of a freelance site from the very depths of my memory. I remember using it when I ordered character art for Lennon a few years back. She'd gotten it in her head that she wanted to write a book, and like the supportive friend I am, I ordered art of the male love interest for her. He was very hot because of course he was.

Why would I order character art and make him ugly?

She never finished writing the book, but at least we had a hot guy to show for it.

I click around, trying to figure out the website before I realize I can post a job.

"Can't hurt," I mutter.

After crafting a description where I try to sound less pathetic and less sorry for myself, I realize the task is hopeless and put it to rest. I post the sad paragraph anyway.

As it turns out, I'm going to be hiring someone to plan me a birthday day.

Just to prove I'm not some weird creep on the internet, I snap a photo of myself and add it as my profile picture. It's a little dark, and I definitely look tired, but it will have to do.

When I hear the door open, I startle like a teenager who is about to be caught watching Peeta Mellark edits in their room at two am.

Which is stupid because who doesn't watch those?

B and Brian make their way into the kitchen where I'm standing, taking in the state of the house.

When B looks around to see no blood, a tidy living room, and a trampoline now properly stored in the closet, she smiles. That is until she spots the three popsicle wrappers decorating the countertop.

"Did you feed her three popsicles?" she asks.

I chuckle, grabbing the wrappers and adding them to the trash. "No," I say. "That was all me. I'm just mourning the loss of my favorite aunt. You're going on a cruise without me. I was only trying to eat my feelings."

She laughs, stepping forward to lean with her elbows on the kitchen island.

"I am sorry, Ellis," she says. "We could try to buy another ticket."

"No!" The word jumps out a bit too quickly, and I try to think of a way to reel it back in. "No," I correct. "It really is okay. I just want you to take a bunch of pictures so I can live vicariously through you. It'll probably be all gross and snowy by then."

Brian moves to the side of the kitchen to retrieve a glass of water, pressing it to the fridge to fill up the cup before taking a long drink.

"Yeah, well, you know," B begins, "winter is my favorite season, so I'll be sad to miss some of it."

"An absolute ice queen," I tease.

Brian chokes on his water, quickly recovering when he finds his wife's withering glare pointed in his direction.

"I might have gotten a little snippy at the restaurant," B admits as an explanation.

I grab my bag from the island, sliding it over one shoulder. "In that case," I say, "I better get going. For one, it's past my bedtime. For two, I'd hate to interrupt your arguing–or the loud and very private playing Eloise informed me about earlier."

Brian's laugh booms across the kitchen and B quickly shushes him. Her cheeks are bright pink when she turns to me, her mouth hanging open like she wants to say something, but she can't for the life of her get herself to think of anything.

"It's fine." I wave a hand in her direction, striding down the hall to the closet to retrieve my coat. "It's not like I don't know how babies are made. My middle school social education was strong. A great friend group ensured my knowledge was top-notch."

B rolls her eyes, trailing behind me as I work my way to the door with my coat now on my body. "Great," she mutters. "I'm a failure as a parent."

"Well," I say. "You can just blame that on Mom for dying. It was a little rude."

"Such dark humor," B responds, but she doesn't stop herself from chuckling. It's been over ten years, and we all have to cope somehow.

She draws me into another warm hug, proving that she's not as icy as she seems. My aunt holds on a moment longer than usual. It's what she does whenever I bring up my mother, and it's somehow uncomfortable and comforting at the same time.

"You smell like coffee," she says before pulling away.

I twist my head around, trying to see the stain on the back of my coat. It's an impossible task, so I obviously fail, but I catch a whiff of espresso and realize I'll need to wash the thing as soon as I get home.

"I had a run-in with a latte," I confess, a smile splitting across my face.

"Getting into fights, too?" she asks. "Honestly, what kind of guardian was I?"

"A great one." I tighten my coat on my body and open the door, allowing the cool night air to whip through the hall.

It isn't until we say our final goodbyes, and I'm pulling away from the house, that I realize I got a message response regarding my post on the freelance site already.

The fact that someone is considering taking the job makes me believe I might not be that pitiful after all.

I think about the three popsicles I ate by myself and the stains on my shirt.

No, nope. Definitely a sad excuse for a human.

<h1 style="text-align:center">Three</h1>

Griffin

After three hours of staring at a computer screen in what is essentially a dark closet, I've decided that I don't even enjoy music anymore.

Which is an absolute shame and honestly a waste of an entire childhood.

I've only been dreaming about doing something with music since conception. How sad is it that one indie artist could squash all those dreams with a single song?

It's not entirely my fault. There's only so much one can do when the song literally sucks ass. It's like the client sent me a giant pile of shit, and I was then expected to somehow salvage it and turn it into the next indie-pop hit.

The task was doomed from the very beginning.

I run my hand down my face, debating every decision I've made while mixing this track, and then decide to fuck it all and call it done.

Grabbing the plastic water bottle from beneath my stool, I take a swig that reminds me the thing has probably been sitting there too long. I wonder if the chemicals from the plastic will kill me before I have to listen to another horrendous song.

Not likely.

The downside to working as an AV tech for a college is that the job is hourly, and colleges take decent winter breaks. Campus is dead. I'm no longer needed, but I can usually make up for the lack of pay with freelance stuff—mixing audio for various artists. When it's good, it's very good. When it's not, I ponder death. Like right now.

I sigh, stretching my legs out underneath the slim desk and pulling out my phone. Despite my distaste for the project I just finished, I decide I should probably look for another job. My apartment isn't going to pay for itself, and sometimes I win the jackpot and get to work on something I love.

A yawn hits me as I glance at the time in the top right corner of the screen, deciding I should probably call it a night. Before I close the tab, a familiar face pops up.

I blink a few times, wondering if I'm seeing correctly as I stare at a picture of coffee-covered parking lot girl. At least, I think it's her, and if my eyes are to be trusted, she posted a job on this freelance site, and it looks like she's local, too.

Clicking on the picture to make it larger by zooming in, I study everything about her. Brown eyes, black hair, a soft smile–she's definitely the girl from the parking lot. The only difference is she's not scowling at me or asking if I was laughing at her–which, unfortunately, I was.

I definitely laughed at her.

"What could she possibly need done?" I mutter before clicking on the job description.

I blink again, my brow furrowing as I read the details. The girl is looking to hire someone to plan her birthday party? Does she have no friends?

"Impossible," I whisper, skimming the last of the details. Aside from being a bit disheveled, somewhat disoriented, and incredibly flustered, there was nothing observably wrong with this woman.

Quite the opposite, actually.

Even so, I'm met with the truth. She wants someone to plan her birthday for two hundred dollars, and color me curious. I want to figure out why.

I tap the icon to send a message, rewriting it at least three times before settling on something.

Me: *Are you looking for an event planner? Will we be required to keep a guest list and invite friends to this event?*

The message still seems like I'm fishing for information about her current friend situation.

I stare at the screen for longer than I'd like to admit before deciding to exit the cave I use for audio and make my way through the apartment to the kitchen, grabbing a package of Oreos from the pantry. I settle on the couch and pull out my phone again, propping my feet on the wooden coffee table.

Still no answer.

Maybe I should have thought of something else to say. My message could have sounded judgmental. She wouldn't have recognized me from my profile picture either because it consists of one singular logo.

Does that make it worse? Should I change the picture?

After spending a ridiculous amount of time overthinking and debating the pros and cons of utilizing a profile picture that features your face, I see a response pop up.

Ellis34: *Friends are out of town, so I'm looking to have something planned for me. Could be literally anything. It just needs to be enjoyable. I saw on your profile that you're local, so that should be easier.*

I look at the package of Oreos and grab another. This isn't my line of work. I have no business planning a birthday bash for this stranger. If she finds out I was the guy that laughed at her in a coffee shop parking lot, I'm sure she will jump to conclusions about me. For example, she will infer that I'm a stalker.

Which I'm not.

It would be an easy two hundred dollars, though.

Me: *What kinds of activities do you enjoy then? Could you send me a bucket list or something?*

The next response comes slowly, and I decide I may actually be going insane thinking about seeing her again.

I pull up her profile picture, noting that it's dimly lit–like it was taken in the middle of the night. I'm not sure what this says about the mystery girl, but when I visualize the coffee sliding off the top of her car again, and landing squarely on her head, I realize she must have had one hell of a day to post this job.

Another message appears.

Ellis34: *Nobody has ever asked me for a bucket list before lol. I'd like to get a tattoo or ride a bull.*

Crashing a wedding has always sounded fun. Sleep beneath the stars, though that would be difficult considering it's December. Maybe see a Broadway play or do something that terrifies me (within reason). I've always wanted to write my own song.

I smile, reading the last item on her list. I could figure something out for that. There's no way she sings as poorly as the last guy.

I tap on her profile picture one more time. What would it hurt? I could use some extra spending money, and I'm sure I could figure it out. This also won't put me in a bad situation with another artist who has next to no talent since my regular clients don't need anything right now.

Me: *When do you want to do this?*

Ellis34: *My birthday's on the twenty-first. I could make the eighteenth, nineteenth, twentieth, or twenty-first work as long as it's in the evening. I'm not picky.*

I put my phone away and grab a third Oreo from the package, shoving it in my mouth just as Simon jumps on the coffee table, a cat getting up to trouble, no doubt.

I lean forward. "What do you think?" I ask, knowing full well the cat gives zero fucks about me or my life. He's just here to beg for dinner. "You think I should do it?"

Simon meows when I pet him behind the ears. I know the little fucker is just asking for food, but I take it as confirmation that I should plan coffee girl a killer birthday.

Grabbing my phone again, I look at the job, and click accept, typing out another message before grabbing the Oreos and heading off toward the cat food.

Me: *Saturday the eighteenth? Five o'clock?*

Four

Ellis

"One can't be responsible for the decisions made at night with a popsicle stain on one's shirt, Lennon." I spin in my chair, grabbing another pretzel from the small bag on my desk. Lennon chuckles on the other end of the line from Minneapolis.

"Actually," she says, "one can."

I huff, leaning back and moving side to side. My entire body is full of anxious energy regarding tomorrow's birthday event with a literal stranger. The guy is local, and he's planning on taking me somewhere as opposed to just telling me where to go and hiring a car. I guess that's why I decided it would be a good idea to call Lennon on my lunch break. I'm not sure why I thought that, though. She's relentless and downright abusive.

"You did this to yourself. You could literally be celebrating your birthday with Ted Bundy."

"Don't say that." My stomach flips, and I shove the bag of pretzels away with a wince. "We are still in the dungeon here. I'm surrounded by the sounds of a furnace that conveniently doesn't heat our part of the office and the dripping of a damp basement."

They attempted to make this strange part of the downstairs look like an office, but I still can't help thinking it's a horror movie scene, and my current situation combined with Lennon's Ted Bundy references? It doesn't help matters.

Rupert walks in, and I watch him duck into the cubicle next to me. My nose wrinkles, knowing that if he's returning from lunch, the scent of tuna is about to waft over the divider and into my space. My nose crinkles prematurely.

I love the guy, but tuna reeks.

"Listen," Lennon starts, breaking my thoughts. "First of all, you're probably going to be able to sue your company for mold exposure or something. You'll be rich, so I'm not concerned about the dungeon. Second, just make sure you meet this strange audio-engineering guy in a public place. You can feel out the vibes and see if he's an axe murderer."

"An axe murderer?" I question, the sound of paper rustling from Rupert's side hitting me just before the scent of tuna and coffee.

Gross.

"All I'm saying is maybe start with coffee, and if it seems like he's planning to peel off your skin and wear it, then flee the premises."

"Again," I state, my tone flat. "You can't say that shit. I'm in the dungeon." I pick up a pen and anxiously click it before I see Rupert's white hair poke around the wall, a scowl etched on his face. Holding my hand up apologetically, I glance at the clock. My lunch is up in two minutes.

"Lennon, I have to go." I sigh, listening to the shuffling in the background. "Are you enjoying your time with your family?" I ask.

"Considering that I'm in the car to get Pedialyte, Pepto, and plain white bread for my mother who has severe food poisoning? No, Ellis, I am not having fun, and I'd much rather be back in Ohio with you for your birthday."

I smile, knowing how much Lennon hates vomit despite her horror movie references. "You'll be fine," I assure, glancing once more at the clock. "And I'll be fine. I might be murdered, but I'm sure you'll plan a killer funeral. Pun intended." I smile, switching my phone to the other ear. "I really do have to go, though."

"Jokes on you if you think I'm planning your funeral. That sounds almost as bad as watching my mother shoot Pedialyte out of her nose because of undercooked chicken. Call me later?"

"Always."

I hang up the phone, considering Lennon's comment about meeting in a public place. At the very least, if I message this guy and tell him I am team coffee first, and he gets upset, then at least I know Lennon was probably right. He was looking to wear my skin. Maybe I should skip the lotion tomorrow.

Technically, my lunch is over, but I type out the quick message, anyway.

Me: *For tomorrow, do you think we could meet up at a coffee shop first?*

The sudden thought that he could ghost me anyway plagues me as I put my phone down and fix my eyes to the computer screen. If he ghosts, maybe I can just buy a bunch of popsicles and make more bad decisions.

"Lennon?" Rupert says as he rolls his chair around. The whiff of tuna is strong enough to knock me out, and I internally curse myself for not buying more gum to share.

My nose wrinkles before I face him. "Yeah, she's visiting family up in Minneapolis for the holidays."

Rupert smiles, the wrinkles at his eyes becoming more pronounced. "Sounds fun, but isn't she missing your birthday, then?"

I sigh, turning to my computer, clicking around–doing anything but acknowledge my sad, sad life. Rupert has been working for the company forever, and while he cannot work his way around a spreadsheet, he somehow kept his job. Honestly, the man should be retired by now.

His presence must be the Universe's way of watching out for me. While the guy is old and smells like tuna, he gives decent advice, is kind, and is also the closest thing I've ever had to a father.

"I have a plan for my birthday. It's kind of like a blind date without any of the romance. Just two strangers–" I trail off, realizing I shouldn't have started explaining this. It sounded better in my head. "I don't really know what we will be doing."

Rupert grunts, folding his arms across his chest. I glance back at him, noting the wrinkled button down and the deep concern on his brow. "Was that what all the axe murderer talk was about? I'm not sure I like the idea of all that. You're meeting a stranger to take you on some adventure?"

I clear my throat, spinning in my chair and sitting up straighter. Maybe if I appear confident, he will trust me to be the adult I am and stop looking at me like a child toddling to his or her death. "It'll be fine. I'll be meeting the guy in a coffee shop–somewhere public. That's what Lennon and I discussed."

Rupert runs a hand down his face as if this conversation aged him five years. I'm surprised he isn't dead. "Okay, Ellie," he says, and something about his tone makes me feel like a scolded teenager. "Okay."

My brow furrows, and I watch as he slides his chair back around, disappearing behind the cubical wall. I'm suddenly more aware of the subtle dripping sound of the basement.

Maybe I should be concerned about this meeting.

"But if anything goes wrong," Rupert says from the other side of the wall. "You call me. I can have my son pick you up or something. You still have my number from when you watched Lola?"

Lola happens to be Rupert's equally ancient chihuahua. He adopted her after his wife died last year to cope with the loss. I dog-sat for him over the summer and got the rundown on his entire life. His son, Joseph, works as a pediatrician and is married with three kids.

"Okay, Rupert," I say, my tone tight. "I still have it."

He rolls around again, glaring at me and pointing a finger. "Don't act upset. I'm only trying to help you be safe."

"I know." I offer him a smile, and something tugs in my chest–just slightly. "I'll call you if anything is amiss."

He disappears again. "Good."

The next time I check my phone isn't until I'm leaving after five, and I'm not sure if the message brings me any more peace or not.

GJPAudio: *Sure. Do you know the one off Oaklawn? Small place with lots of plants in the window.*

<h1 style="text-align:center">Five</h1>

Griffin

The door opens behind me as I finish putting my laptop in my backpack.

Before winter break, the college university I work for typically hosts a final assembly to send students off campus. Despite how it sounds, most of the student body shows up because the college president happens to be a very entertaining speaker. It's practically free stand-up, and I don't mind running sound for it, although I prefer when the campus has guests show up for concerts. That's when I get to do the real shit.

"What are you up to over break?" Noah leans against the door, his black hair neatly styled, and his brown sweater screaming the words *English Professor.*

I chuckle, scanning his outfit before pulling my phone out of my backpack. "The glasses new?" I ask, rolling my tongue along my cheek. "Or is that just a part of the professor aesthetic?"

"Shut up." Noah folds his arms across his chest, fighting the smile threatening to break free. "They're new, and yes, I bought them because they fit with the dark academia theme."

I lean back in the chair with my phone on my lap, pulling the hood of my sweatshirt up and putting my hands on my head. "Dark academia theme? You mean your very elaborate scheme to get women in bed with you?"

Noah cocks a brow. "Says the man who does his little music shit on the side. Nobody's fooled." He grins, drumming his fingers on his bicep. "Are you ever going to quit this job? You do enough work for indie artists. I'm sure someone would take you on the road. You'd be good at touring."

My stomach feels like lead as I stare at him, the corners of my lips pulling into a frown. "Not likely."

I thought about it once—going on tour and running audio across the country. In fact, it was somewhat of a dream before my brother passed. Something about losing a family member while you're still in highschool—a family member who was so young—changes the trajectory of your life.

Family became more important.

Home became more important.

Dreams be damned. I'm happy with what I do for the most part.

Noah bends down, retrieving a bag from his feet. "Your mom requested more pho. I told her I'd stop by and bring it to you, but you'll need to move fast. My mother doesn't want it spoiling."

I smile, grabbing the bag from him and placing it near my backpack. "Of course." I chuckle. "I should have expected it. Ma tried the pho recipe, and it was terrible. The woman can paint, but can't cook to save her life. I'm sorry she's resorted to begging your poor mother for dinner."

Noah adjusts the leather satchel strapped across his chest. "It's no problem."

I finally pick up my phone to see a message from coffee shop girl. I can't help the way my palms instantly turn sweaty–the way my stomach churns with nerves.

This entire thing was probably a stupid idea.

Ellis34: *Oaklawn sounds good. I'll just meet you there at five?*

One corner of my mouth turns up at the message.

"Who is it?" Noah asks, pushing his glasses higher up his nose. "Or should I say, who is *she*?"

"No one."

His brows raise, his brown eyes scolding. There's no reason to hide it other than planning a stranger's birthday sounds completely idiotic. But considering I still haven't fully planned what we will do, it can't hurt to get some advice.

"Freelance work," I offer, knowing damn well he realizes it isn't just another mixing job. "Some girl wanted someone to plan her birthday party. Two-hundred bucks."

"Event planning. That's an interesting change in pace. Is she hot?"

I run my tongue along my teeth, refusing to answer and definitely refusing to make eye contact.

"Okay, so that explains why you took the job. Where are you taking her?"

I stand up, grabbing my backpack and the food off the floor. I'll need to stop by my parents on my way home. "Not sure yet."

"You're literally an idiot." Noah chuckles, the smile dancing on his lips.

"I asked her for a bucket list. I'll probably just pick something off there." I shrug my backpack over my shoulder, slowly making my way to the door. Noah follows out the door, and I turn to lock up the sound booth behind me.

"So, skydiving in December?"

I shake my head. "Wasn't on the list."

Noah holds out his hand expectantly. "Well," he says. "Let's see it then. The list, I mean."

I pull up my messages with *Ellis34* and hand the phone over. He skims the list with a smile on his face. "Oh shit. You know that one professor in the biology department is getting married tomorrow at The Outlook? Real black-tie-level event. You guys could totally crash a wedding."

"You don't think that would be ridiculous?"

Noah shrugs, considering for a moment. "Nah, it could be fun. Angie is really uptight anyway and deserves to have someone crash her big day. I'll get immense joy knowing you got to attend. Make sure you give me a play-by-play."

The thought turns over in my mind. *Technically,* crashing a wedding is on the list of things she wants to do. It could be a fun birthday adventure–something different.

We head down the stairs and out of the auditorium, and I tuck my phone in my pocket. By now, most of the students have cleared out, and the parking lot is nearly empty.

Noah stops, tossing a thumb over his shoulder in the other direction. "I parked by the English building, but you keep me updated on what you decide." His face splits into a wide smile. "And please know that I am literally on my knees begging and pleading for you to crash Angie's wedding."

I laugh, muttering, "Sure," before walking my way to my car.

When I get inside the Jeep, I stare at my phone, opening the message thread again.

Me: *Oaklawn coffee shop at five, so you can see if I'm legit or out to unalive you.*

I chuckle before second-guessing myself completely and sending another message.

Me: *I'm not, by the way.*

Me: *I'm not trying to unalive you. I do freelance stuff a lot. You can look at my profile. I'm verified and have a ton of great ratings.*

I wince, barreling on.

Me: *It's also important to note that I didn't type that with the tone of a pompous asshat. I'm not trying to brag about my ratings.*

Me: *Though they are good. That's why I was directing your attention there.*

Me: *I suppose it doesn't matter. This isn't audio production, anyway.*

I rest my head on the steering wheel, desperately trying to find some button that allows me to unsend the ridiculous thread of messages I just accosted this poor girl with.

Jesus.

I watch the words *typing* appear under her name and immediately consider throwing up on the sidewalk. She read them—all of them.

Ellis34: *Lol*
Ellis34: *Serial killer status tbd*

Starting the car, I pull out of the parking lot and internally cringe for the entire drive to my parents' house.

This was definitely a bad idea.

Six

Ellis

It's safe to say that my stomach feels like I just slammed two tacos from Taco Bell, and I am both lactose intolerant and have a bad history of IBS.

None of those things are true. Though I do feel like I'm going to throw up while I stand in line at the coffee shop, checking my phone and looking around the room like the worst spy to ever exist.

Lennon: *You'll be fine.*
Lennon: *But if not, nice knowing ya.*

I roll my eyes, shoving my phone in my back pocket as I take one step closer to the counter. I'm next in line, and I haven't even decided what I'm getting. Deciding that today isn't the time to debate a new drink, I settle on a caramel latte just before glancing back at the door.

Bells rattle on the glass as a tall man walks into the room. The coffee shop on Oaklawn is small—really small, and he's tall enough that he seems to eat up most of the space as well as the air. Running a hand through his black hair, his eyes flick around the few tables scattered in the shop. He adjusts the jean jacket he has over his black sweatshirt.

My brow furrows, memories rattling around in my head until my mind lands on one.

"Oh my god," I whisper, spinning around to face the counter. It's the guy from the parking lot like three days ago. I knew going to the same coffee shop was a bad decision.

Wiping my palms on my jeans, I step forward and offer a warm smile to the barista in an effort to ignore him. "I'll just get a medium caramel latte. Hot." Nervous energy buzzes through my body as I tap my debit card on the counter, waiting for Dorothy—as it shows on her nametag—to ring up my order. It's almost like I can feel his presence looming over the few people behind me.

When I scoot over to wait for my drink and let the next customer order, I risk a glance back. The guy is staring ahead, eyes fixed on the menu on the wall. His lips are pulled into a firm and unamused line, looking like the embodiment of that emoji with the two round eyes and the straight line for a mouth. Not friendly at all.

Which checks out after he laughed at me when I spilled my coffee on myself.

My cheeks flush with embarrassment, and I hear Dorothy call out my drink order.

"Thanks," I say, keeping my head down and making my way toward the window to sit down next to no less than five million plants decorating the airy space.

When the sage green chair scratches against the light hardwood, I wince, trying to keep the attention off myself. There's no way he will remember me, right? He couldn't.

Pulling out my phone, I search up the messages between me and Mr. Great Ratings and Certainly Not an Unaliver.

Me: *I'm sitting at the table by the window. Please use my profile picture for reference. I'm not catfishing you, and as you probably guessed, my name is Ellis.*

I tap my finger on the wooden surface of the table and pick up my drink in the other hand, sipping the warm caffeine that will absolutely not increase my anxiety in any way whatsoever.

The sun is already setting over the city, streaks of pink and orange painted across the sky, and for a moment, I almost forget it's winter. Then my eyes drag to the lifeless trees, the brown grass, and crumpled leaves, and I remember how ugly winter in Ohio is before the first snow.

"Ellis?"

A deep voice–somehow soft–catches me off guard, and I turn to look at who I presume to be *GJPAudio*. Maybe Lennon was right. It really is like a horror movie. My heartbeat is in my ears, and I'm turning my head slowly. I can almost feel the sweat beading at my temple as I strain to glance at my murderer.

Parking lot comedian boy.

I blink up at him–certain that I'm glitching. But there he is with his clear hazel eyes, thick black lashes, and cleanly shaven face.

Did he call me Ellis? How would he know–

Oh god.

"This is not real," I mutter, so low it's almost inaudible.

The guy just stares at me, his expression still stone serious as it was when he walked in. I'm not sure why he looks like that–all pissed off. Maybe this is revenge for me calling him rude. I'm not sure he even heard that.

"Sorry, what?" he asks, looking–well, not friendlier. He holds a coffee in one veined hand, his black hair messier up close, but in an irritatingly handsome way.

"Are you–" I trail off, waiting for him to fill in the gaps and desperately hoping that GJPAudio is not him, and he is not that.

I'm starting to think that *I'm* the one being catfished.

"GJPAudio," he answers. *No, he is not.* "Well, my name's actually Griffin."

Do I ask him to sit down? Do I tell him to leave?

I stand up awkwardly, pulling at the oversized corduroy flannel over my cream turtleneck. The chair screeches across the floor, and I throw my hand at him like an aggressive car salesman who just made the deal of a lifetime.

"Ellis," I say. He takes my hand, staring where I'm shaking his limb for what I assume to be an inappropriate amount of time because his brows furrow, and he isn't looking away from the handshake and–

This was a terrible idea.

"You already know that," I realize. "You called me Ellis a minute ago." I disconnect my hand from his, the warmth still lingering on my skin. Impulsively I wipe it on my jeans like he has a virus, and I know he sees. Honestly, my palms have just been really sweaty lately. If he's offended, it doesn't show aside from the unamused emoji face he still has going on. "I'm so sorry," I say. "I'm actually pretty nervous about this."

Something that I can only describe as a miracle happens. Griffin looks down, a breathy laugh escaping as he smiles. It's like the expression changes his entire face–making him look far kinder than a rude man who laughs at struggling women in parking lots. It's the kind of shy smile that makes me question my reality and helps my shoulders to relax infinitesimally.

He looks–*nice*.

"I know," he says, his eyes meeting mine–green and brown with a touch of humor. That hazel color looks more interesting when he doesn't look like he loathes the world and everyone in it.

I smile, matching his expression as he gestures to the table. "Why don't we just sit and drink coffee? You can complete a full background check before we start focusing on you."

"Focusing on me?" I question, my head tilting to the side.

His smile disappears, his nose scrunching in confusion as he looks away briefly. "This is for your birthday, right? I have a whole thing planned." He licks his lips, shaking his head once as if he thought of something else to add, but skipped it.

I chuckle nervously, moving around the table to pull out his chair and immediately realizing that out of the two of us, based on my behavior, I'm more likely to go off murdering kind strangers and wearing their skin. "Right," I say. "My birthday, yes."

He makes a singular sound—one that hints at a laugh but isn't quite there before sitting in the seat I pulled out as I hustle to the other side of the table to sit across from him.

"Like I said, I'm just nervous." I bring the coffee to my lips trying to find something to do with my hands that doesn't involve selling cars to this man or pulling out his chair like I'm seventeen and taking him to a pre-prom dinner with my aunt's credit card.

When he doesn't say anything, a desperate need to fill the silence creeps up my throat. "You're the guy that laughed at me when I spilled my coffee a few days ago."

That smile breaks free again, and he leans forward, his elbows on the table as he grips the coffee with both hands. A hint of a tattoo peaks out by his wrist, and I wonder if I should ask him about what others he may have. This will help me identify him if I have to call Rupert and tell him to send his son to pick me up—though something about Griffin's presence tells me that won't be necessary.

Lennon would call it *vibes*.

I bet his family and friends pay good money to see him smile like this–it sure as hell beats the RBF he supported earlier.

"Sorry about that." He leans back again, his knee bouncing beneath the table–the only indication that he's nervous too. "It just snuck out."

"The laugh?" I press my lips together before continuing. "I was having a rough day." I don't offer any more information, just wait for him to respond, but he simply nods before bringing his own coffee up to his mouth and drinking.

The silence stretches, and I begin to wonder how much this guy gets out of the house. "So, what did you have planned?"

Griffin clears his throat, shifting in his seat. "Right, well, I know you wrote about the song thing, and I'm actually an audio engineer." His brow furrows. "You could see that on my profile. I do production stuff on the side. I really work as an AV tech for one of the colleges a little ways east. Anyway, I thought about doing the song thing because I have everything we would need. A keyboard, well-treated room. Diffusion and acoustic treatments, various outboard gear. I also love music." He pauses, blinking at me, and I know he must register the confused expression on my face. I knew about two of the words he used in that long run-on sentence. "Never mind," he says quickly. "I was thinking we'd write a song from your list, but I didn't want to weird you out by taking you to my apartment. We're doing something else."

"Okay," I drag the word out, running my finger along the lid of my coffee cup. "What is the something else?"

"Well, you're going to need to change your outfit."

I look down at my outfit with my brows pulled together. When I look back up, that smile returns. I can see the excitement in his eyes, and something about it makes me feel it, too. One corner of my mouth turns up. "I didn't bring extra clothes."

"We can stop at a thrift store and get you something. You'll need to wear a dress–a nice one. I'll have to change, too. I have a suit in the car." He takes another drink, and I watch the column of his throat when he swallows, quickly averting my eyes because I'm not blind, and when he smiles like that something warm rushes through my blood.

"What are we *doing*, though?" Getting this guy to talk is like trying to lasso a grain of sand–impossible.

When I look back, his smile widens, soft eyes looking down at me from the other side of the table. "We're going to crash a wedding."

My eyes widen, my heart suddenly pounding in my chest. "What?" I screech. I'm wringing my hands under the table, listening to the soft chuckle that passes through his lips as he takes in my wild expression.

"It was on the list," he explains.

I don't say anything. He's right–I did ask for this. In fact, I'm the one that gave him the list. For my entire life, I've been so used to doing the right thing–the reasonable thing. I've bent over backwards, stressing myself out about what other people need and how I can make their existence on this planet easier. I think that maybe at this moment, it's time for me to do something different–to think a little less.

"It was," I admit.

The look on his face threatens to take me right out, and I decide that I'm going to stop thinking–stop worrying–at least for tonight.

Griffin's eyes cut to mine, glittering with something like adventure. "Happy Birthday, Ellis."

Seven

Griffin

When I pull up to the thrift store, I see Ellis already parked suspiciously far away from the entrance and sitting in her car on her phone. I wonder who she's texting and if she's giving them a detailed description of my appearance in case she goes missing.

I have no plans to kidnap the woman and decided to prove it by saying I could drive her, or she could drive herself. I figured giving her the choice would make me seem less crazy.

Not that I'm crazy.

She chose to take her own car, and I guess something about me not tying her up and shoving her in my Jeep gave her a good read on my character. How did she phrase it?

Definitely not Ted Bundy vibes?

When I get out of my vehicle after parking a *normal* distance from the entrance, she looks up, smiles, pockets her phone, and kills the engine.

And now, the entire universe waits for her to cross mountains and valleys–to walk through the desert before finding her way to her destination.

I shove my hands in my jacket pockets to fight against the biting chill in the air. It's not unreasonably cold. In fact, I think my weather app said forty-two this morning. If I know anything about Ohio, though, I know that tomorrow could be a polar vortex, and the following day could be sunny and seventy-five. It's a real shit show.

The truth is, I'm putting tremendous amounts of pressure on myself to make this day great for her. Noah's assumptions aside, birthdays are a big deal–especially in my family. I'm close with my parents, and with Skylar, my sister, even though she lives in New York City.

Long story short, nobody is around for her birthday, so I have an opportunity to be somebody–for her–at least for the day.

Ellis approaches with a gentle smile dancing on her lips. Her cheeks are tinted pink from the cold, her dark hair rising around her with the gentle breeze.

My eyes catch on the faint freckle on her temple before meeting her eyes–dark amber like the sun during the golden hour–just before shades of purple and pink paint the sky.

"Why did you park in Europe?" I ask when she gets close enough to stand in front of me. She has to look up and crosses her arms as if she's freezing. I briefly considered giving her my jacket. She isn't wearing a coat–just a cream shirt and some brown button-up over it.

I decide the jacket thing is too date-like, but continue to question that at least twelve times before making my decision. It's her birthday, and I'm watching her torture herself with Ohio weather, but we'll be inside soon, anyway.

Ellis looks back across the parking lot briefly before her eyes meet mine. "I didn't want anyone to hit my car."

A half-smile tugs at the corner of my mouth. *Cute,* I think, but I keep my tone casual and my thoughts to myself. "You know there are still cars driving in Europe, right?"

She gestures to the parking lot, looking around and making a show of it. "Looks like there are considerably fewer cars in Europe, as you can see. My chances of someone scratching the paint are far lower."

I chuckle, nodding toward the door without saying anything, encouraging her to follow me.

She does.

We stroll toward the store nestled in a small strip mall near the coffee shop. The only sounds that follow us are the scuff of our shoes on asphalt and the gentle sound of wind. I risk a glance sideways at her, noting that the breeze is still carrying stray strands of black hair around her face. She swipes at them, but it doesn't do anything to keep her vision clear.

I smile but try to hide it.

I can't make her think I have Ted Bundy vibes.

"Where is the wedding?" she asks as we approach the door.

I rush forward to open it, allowing her to walk in first before answering. "The Outlook. It's a fancy golf course about forty minutes away. Is that too far?"

"That's like really fancy," she says. "Are you sure we will find a dress here? You said you have a suit."

"I think we will." I check the time on my watch. "The wedding starts in an hour and a half, so we better start looking."

I make my way toward the far wall where dresses hang on disorganized racks. Ellis rushes forward, practically jumping in front of me.

She immediately yanks things off hangers and throws them over her arm. I watch her–somewhat mystified. "You sure are being very critical when it comes to looking for a gown," I say, one brow raised.

Her glare cuts to me, slicing me in half in a way that warms my chest. "To be frank, you didn't exactly give lots of time. I'm just going to try on as many things as possible."

"Okay." I move clothes aside, assaulted by orange and pink and some ugly floral pattern that reminds me of my grandmother's bedsheets. "You want me to pick a few things?"

"I think you should help, yes." She's focused, forehead wrinkled in concentration as she pulls a teal dress down from the hanger and drapes it over her already full pile.

I can't help the breathy laugh that escapes. Maybe Noah was right. It would be fucking stupid to say I didn't find her attractive, but I won't admit that or think about it. Again, I'm trying to distance myself from Ted Bundy.

I find a black dress that seems decent and pull it off the hanger, sifting through the aisle to add a gray dress and some bright orange jumpsuit. The jumpsuit is objectively ugly. It's exactly why I picked the thing.

"So," I start, moving to stand next to her as she furiously looks through the gowns on her arm. "What do you do for work?"

"I actually collect human bodies and wear the skin." She looks up, her brown eyes sparkling with amusement, when she notices my blank stare. "Kidding," she says. "I work in marketing. It's very–" She clears her throat, glancing back down at the dresses when her brows stitch together. "Stable," she finishes.

"Sounds like a true passion for you."

Those dark amber eyes whip to mine. "It's enjoyable," she defends. "I enjoy it."

"I don't believe you."

Her eyes narrow, dipping to notice the smile I'm holding in before she pats the pile of dresses she's carrying. If she carried anymore, I'm afraid she would topple over. "Alright," she says. "Time to try these on." She glances at the three pitiful clothing items I've collected for her. "I'm not boring, by the way."

"I never said you were."

"It was implied with the whole marketing discussion." Her eyes cut to the orange jumpsuit. "I'll try that one first." Ellis snatches the garment out of my hands like she's determined to make it her outfit for the wedding. "If only to prove that I am not boring."

I let the smile loose when she turned around to waltz into the dressing rooms. I follow along, seating myself on a random bench and pulling out my phone as she disappears into the stall.

Stretching an arm behind my head, I rub the back of my neck nervously. It's the only indication I give to the fact that my stomach has been swirling and twisting since the moment I saw her in the coffee shop.

I really want this to go well, and I'm painfully aware of the fact that it might not.

When I thumb through my phone, I find a text from Noah.

Noah: *How's your hot date?*

Me: *Not a date*

Noah: *But hot? What have you talked about? What are you wearing?*

Me: *Decline to answer. Marketing. Khakis.*

Noah: *Listen, for a guy who has the whole indie-music thing going for him, you're really terrible with women. Maybe you should try becoming an English Professor and wearing glasses.*

Noah: *Also . . . Khakis?*

I glance down at my black jeans and huff a laugh. A loud noise sounds from the dressing room has me snapping my gaze up.

I don't even have time to respond or ask a question.

"I'm fine!" Ellis shouts from inside the room.

"Glad to hear it."

I look back at my phone.

Me: *I'm not trying to pick this girl up.*
Noah: *Famous last words*

The door to the dressing room opens, and Ellis strides out in the bright orange, silk jumpsuit, her dark hair spilling around her shoulders. It's sleeveless–the absolute worst considering the temperature–and as previously anticipated, it's ugly.

Not Ellis.

She's not ugly.

Just the outfit.

"It smells like salami," she says, and I burst out laughing, shoving my phone into my pocket.

"You look–" My words fizzle out. I don't want her to think I'm insulting her.

"Like a chic prison inmate? Like I skinned an Oompa Loompa and took up fashion design?" My laugh comes out harder than I expected, booming through the entire thrift store. I'm certain at least four old ladies and the young mom with no less than five million teacups in her cart turn around to look at us. I don't bother being embarrassed. "Yes," Ellis insists. "I know, Finn!" she huffs.

"Unfortunately, the other options are ugly too, and we are running out of time. Where's the black dress you found?"

I lift it up from where it sits next to me on the bench, and she moves forward, tripping on the too-long legs of her prison uniform before snatching it out of my hands and disappearing.

"Nobody calls me Finn," I inform, listening to her shuffle around and watching the black dress fly up and settle across the top of the door.

"Well, I do!" she says. There's a brief pause before she speaks again. "Oh, my god."

I hear the panic in her voice and instantly stand up, moving closer to the door. "What?" I ask, not really knowing what to do with my hands–or my feet–or anything.

"Oh, my god!" she repeats, a little louder, and I risk a gentle knock.

"Ellis, what is it?"

"The salami suit from hell is stuck! I blame you!" There's no real heat to her words, but I can tell she's still working to get the thing off by the sounds of fabric and frantic movement.

I chuckle, leaning closer to the door as if it'll help her hear me. "Use the buttons."

"It's a zipper, and it's not going down. This is a disaster."

I grunt. "Your birthday? A disaster? Not on my watch."

The door cracks open, and she pokes her head around from the other side, looking back and forth like she's about to commit a crime.

That's when she grabs my arm and drags me into the dressing room with her.

"Is this legal?" I question.

"You have to help me. I can't be stuck in this suit. You planned this day, and I'm paying you good money, Finn. Fix the zipper."

My mouth quirks up at the corner when she calls me Finn, noting that I'm smiling an awful lot in her presence. She turns around, pulling her hair over one shoulder, and I think I malfunction for a moment. "I'm not Ted Bundy," I say, lifting my hands to the half-undone zipper at her back, lingering and scared to touch her.

"I know! Just help me out of this thing."

I carefully touch the zipper, giving it a gentle tug. It doesn't move. "Definitely stuck."

She laughs, and something in me relaxes at the fact that she isn't angry–she's still laughing.

I tug a little harder. "You don't have a boyfriend that's going to kill me for undressing you in this Goodwill, do you?"

She laughs again–a soft breathy sound–and I pull at the fabric, trying to get it loose from the zipper so I can slide the thing down. My heart pounds in my chest as I wait for her to answer and try not to think about what I'm doing or the soft feel of her skin beneath my fingertips.

"That was a loaded question," she says just as I get the thing to move. With each slide, I can see more of her back, and it is in no way unpleasant.

Not even a little.

I bite on the side of my cheek, my entire body becoming warm, but I keep my tone cool. "Was it a loaded question?"

When she shakes her head gently, I'm thankful she's still turned around and can't see me because my face is beet red. I'm sure of it. "Yes!"

Getting my newly diagnosed rosacea under control, I answer her. "It wasn't."

She spins, glaring up at me in a way that has that damn smile pulling at my lips. She doesn't let up, and the smirk grows wider. Something about the look in her eye makes me want to keep goading her. "I'm gaslighting you."

She sighs. "Finally." Her eyes sparkle in the harsh dressing room lights–they're the kind of lights that make people hate themselves as they try on new clothes. Everyone looks ugly in these lights. It's a biblical truth. It makes me question if the girl in front of me is even human because dressed in a silk orange jumpsuit that smells like salami without a properly functioning zipper, she still looks good. Same as she did with coffee all over the back of her coat.

"Finally, a man who admits it." Her tone is teasing, and I can't help how it draws me in.

I lean forward, just slightly, smelling something floral–like spring in December. My nose wrinkles. It's definitely mixed with the scent of deli meat, though. "I'm anything if not self-aware," I say with a smug smirk.

Her eyes flick between mine for a moment, arms holding the front of the jumpsuit in place. My mind briefly recalls that the entire back is undone, and all of that skin was bare. I don't linger on that thought or the fact that it indicates a missing bra. I don't think about it for a second.

"No," she says. "The answer is no. I don't have a boyfriend."

The joy I feel is unmatched, and I internally curse Noah. Then I see the question in her eyes, and I can't help but hope. "Go on," I tease. "Ask your loaded question."

Her face falls, arms still clutching the fabric at her chest. "I'd prefer if you just answered."

I keep my face straight, shrugging. "I have hundreds of girl-friends." She blinks at me. "Because I work in music."

I wait, letting her brow furrow before putting her out of her misery.

"I'm kidding," I offer. "I have none."

She lifts a brow. "Not a single one?"

Shoving my hands in my pockets, I take a step back to keep a respectful distance from her. "Not a single one at the moment. It's rather scandalous for me to be in here. I'm known as a perfect gentleman, usually."

"Well, Finn,"

"Again, nobody calls me that."

"*Finn*, I don't want to be the woman to tarnish your reputation. Get out of here. We've already established I look terrible in prison orange, and I smell of salami and confinement."

I chuckle, glancing toward the ground as I sneak out of the dress-ing room. When I look around the store, I see one of the old women scowling in my direction.

Whatever she thought we were doing, she was completely wrong, but I can't help the way my mind thinks about it–if only for a moment.

As I sit on the bench, I choose to focus on a different trait instead.

Again, I don't want to be Ted Bundy.

I whip out my phone to text Noah.

Me: *She's really funny.*

Eight

Ellis

I t's almost insulting how much fun I'm having.

Something about Griffin's presence—the excitement of not knowing what's coming next—it feels like being let free after a long period of confinement. It reminds me of the orange jumpsuit, honestly.

I've spent so much of my life nervous about what I owe others for my existence. While I know that thought is wrong, as soon as I think about it, I can't help but consider the truth of it.

I've fought to do the right thing–the *safe* thing–the responsible thing. I spend my days working in the dungeon because I selected a college major that made sense and would support me financially. I had no interest in marketing, and somehow Griffin could see right through it.

I have exactly one close friend, and I spend my days hanging out with her or watching Eloise.

My life is certifiably plain and very–adult.

Maybe Griffin was right about the job. His comments poked at this weird *thing* inside of me. Nobody's ever drawn it into question before–not really.

Being with him feels the same way it feels when I work on my sketches–like losing myself in something, and not worrying what other people will think about it.

I tried on a salami suit, for crying out loud, and I barely even knew the guy!

I don't think I've worn anything that bright in–

Ever?

I decided the vibes were right, and when he didn't make a pass at me in the dressing room, I mentally agreed to let him drive me to the wedding venue.

On the ride there, we talked more about our jobs and close friends. I avoided family, for now. I didn't want to spring a sob story onto him.

I also learned that Griffin has a cat named Simon, that he really meant it when he said nobody called him Finn, but he's okay if I do. And I learned his job is incredibly techy–though I kind of got that impression at the coffee shop when he listed equipment I've never heard of.

For all I know, the guy was speaking Latin.

And unfortunately, I took French in high school.

When he parks the car at The Overlook, nerves spark through my body–sending little electric bolts of energy to all my limbs. My legs won't stop shaking, and my entire body feels like a bomb about to explode.

Somehow, I can't keep the smile off my face.

"Ready?" he asks, his deep voice drawing me out of my thoughts. I look over at him in his suit, looking like he belongs with all the guests walking toward the large brick building–painted white with ivy crawling up the sides. Everything is carefully manicured and seated on top of a large hill.

The Overlook is right.

The place is fancy, and I look down at the black dress I'm wearing, hoping we won't get caught doing this, and hoping that I look half as decent as the stranger sitting next to me.

The whole thing feels like waiting in line for a rollercoaster, and after an hour of standing, you're finally seeing the line move, and realizing that you could die–you *might* die. It's actually more likely that you would die, but you can't get the thrill out of your blood.

"How are we going to do this?" I ask, and I'm sure he can sense the nerves in my voice–a little breathless, to be honest.

I try to discreetly adjust the top of my dress, the sweetheart neckline and off-the-shoulder sleeves complimenting my figure far better than the orange jumpsuit. Despite our time crunch, I'd say Griffin did an outstanding job picking something out from the thrift store. He even paid for it.

All seven dollars.

I'm certain he's rich.

Or he's just using the two-hundred bucks he got when he accepted the job I posted, but I don't linger on that thought long.

I look across the center console again. He *definitely* looks like he could fit in with this black-tie event.

We stopped at a gas station for him to change, and I don't think I've ever seen a man come out of a gas station bathroom looking better. Usually, they just look uncomfortable and like they're trying to fight off the burning in their butthole from intense road trip diarrhea.

If Griffin had that issue, I wouldn't know.

"Don't worry," he says, opening his door with a wide smile splitting his face. "I have a plan."

He rushes around to my side of his car and opens my door for me to carefully step out as I run my hands along the skirt of my gown. The fabric hugs my legs–my butt–and somewhere deep inside, the feral woman at my core decides she would like someone to take notice.

Did he notice in the dressing room?

Obviously not because I smelled like a deli counter.

I close the door, watching as guests start filing into the building from all around. The sun is setting, and I'm wondering why the couple chose to have an evening wedding. Aren't these things typically hosted over an entire day?

"What's this glorious plan you have?" I ask, returning his smile when I look up at him. He offers his arm, and my stomach does a weird little dip.

Griffin leans in, eyeing the people around us, too far to hear our conversation as we approach the doors. "Listen very carefully," he starts. "We are attending as friends of the bride and groom."

I roll my tongue along my cheek. "Naturally."

"Yes, naturally. We met them during their romantic getaway in Kansas. We were honeymooning there at the time."

"Kansas?" I question, fighting the urge to laugh. "What's in Kansas? Why did we honeymoon in Kansas?"

We get closer to the door, and Griffin keeps his voice down the closer we get.

Strangers are staring at us, and I suddenly feel like they can see right through this ridiculous charade. They can't know? How intimate is this wedding, anyway?

Oh my god, what if they know?

"Tornados and bicycles," he says, as if it's an appropriate answer. Which it's not.

"Okay, so we met them while biking in a Kansas tornado for our honeymoon. Got it. What do I call you?"

"Your husband," Griffin answers. "But during the moments when your chest swells with ardent love and affection, you call me Stuart."

I laugh so hard I snort through my nose, and one woman across the way glares at me, judgment painted on her face. "Is that your name for the duration of this event?" I ask.

"No, it's the name of the man you actually love, but he left you at the altar, and then you settled for me."

I can see the wicked grin dancing on his lips as he keeps his eyes forward. Ushers help guests into the building, guiding them through the gilded hallway and past large wooden doors where I assume the reception will be held.

"This is very complicated," I finally admit. "And somewhat depressing. I thought it was supposed to be my birthday? Why are you giving me unrequited love on my birthday?"

"Don't worry," Griffin answers. "Stuart is the groom. You get to stop the ceremony, and I promise you'll have a happy ending."

I swat at him, leaning in slightly with my arm still threaded through his. He smells like expensive cologne–amber and something spicy. "No, it's not," I say. There's no way the groom's name is actually Stuart.

"It's not." He's smiling down at me, and I recall, for a moment, the way he looked when he first walked into the coffee shop. There's no sign of that version of him now. There's something brighter about this version of Griffin–like treasure just waiting to be uncovered.

I've never wanted to be a pirate more in my life.

"We can just make this up as we go," Griffin states. "It'll be fun."

When we get to the door, ushers promptly escort us to two white chairs at the back of the bride's side in the massive ballroom Undetected like little spies, I'm inclined to believe him.

• • • • •• • •• • • •

My entire body is buzzing. The whole ceremony felt like a secret mission–like I was trying to steal the Declaration of Independence.

Griffin assured me that the ceremony was the easy part. Everyone had their eyes on Angie, some biology professor from Finn's college where he works, and her husband–*not* Stuart.

"I was rather disappointed," I say when we stand up, moving toward the large hall closer to the entrance. A few dozen people dressed in all black descend on the ceremony space, no doubt converting it into something usable for the reception. "This wasn't Stuart's wedding at all. Now you've really given me unrequited love for my birthday."

Griffin steps forward, his eyes lighted. "I just couldn't lose my wife. Did Kansas mean nothing to you?"

I chuckle. "My dear husband, Kansas meant *everything*. We chased tornadoes. It was very memorable."

One corner of his mouth pulls up. It's soft and teasing–another smile for me to enjoy. "Good," he says. "Now comes the fun part. Let's go lie to some people."

He grabs my hand and drags me out of the ballroom. My heart is pounding with anticipation, the heels I picked up at the thrift store clicking across the white tile floors. "We are so going to hell," I comment, and just as we make it to the entrance of the hall, Griffin looks back at me and gives me my other favorite smile. The one he showed me at the coffee shop.

Lennon is not going to believe any of this.

Nine

Griffin

I'm trying to be relaxed walking through the crowd of strangers dressed in their best clothes for this ridiculous wedding. Every nerve in my body is on edge, afraid to mess it up, but when I look back at Ellis and see the joy on her face, the way she lights up in the name of adventure, none of those nerves bother me–not a single one.

We mingle in the hall during the cocktail hour, and I grab two glasses of champagne off a tray floating by. Scanning the large hall at the entrance to The Overlook, I find Ellis standing alone, eyes wide and looking around the room to take in the white tiles, gold accents, and large chandelier hanging over the center of the space. She's pulling at the long sleeves of her gown, and I fight the urge to dip my eyes lower.

I walk up behind her with the glasses. "Here," I say, and she turns around, eyes still wide until she notes the drink I'm holding in front of her. "Maybe it'll calm your nerves," I supply. "Do you even like champagne? Do you drink?" I can't help the way the questions rattle something inside of me, reminding me that despite how easy she is to talk to, I still know next to nothing about her.

She works in marketing. She isn't afraid of ridiculous jumpsuits or pulling strangers into dressing rooms.

Or maybe she is. This entire birthday thing seems out of the norm—it's certainly out of the norm for me, but I like being around her. I like it a fucking lot.

She takes the glass, smelling its contents before looking back at me. "I *do* drink, and I do like champagne but—"

I raise a brow. "What?"

Ellis leans forward, lowering her voice to a harsh whisper. "We are crashing this wedding, Finn. Isn't this like, I don't know? *Stealing*?"

I take a drink, holding her gaze and watching her scowl at my lack of an answer. The champagne is on the sweeter side. Thank God it's not terrible, because if I were being honest, I was only drinking it to prove a point—to challenge her. Though she is right, it is stealing. She did pay me two hundred dollars for this. Maybe I can leave a bit of cash as a gift—a wedding present for the couple.

I nod toward the glass delicately clasped in her hand. "Drink it, and I'm sure you'll stop worrying."

She hesitates for a moment–like she's weighing the consequences before shrugging and bringing the glass to her lips.

I smirk, nudging her with my arm. "Don't worry, I'll leave a tip for the bride and groom."

When she takes a deep breath, I see her finally relax.

Definitely the type to follow the rules, then.

My eyes fix on her, trying to make all her puzzle pieces fit together. I want to see the full picture of Ellis, and I'm willing to work for it, too. She's funny, I know that and told Noah as much. She's anxious about parking cars, and works in marketing but doesn't seem to enjoy it.

I'm busy listing the things I've learned when a high-pitched voice interrupts my thoughts, drawing our attention to the blonde stranger now standing in front of us.

"Hey," she says. "I'm Cassidy. Cass for short." The petite woman is looking right at us–expecting some kind of response, and I try to settle the spike of adrenaline that runs through my blood. *Cass* tosses a strand of blonde hair over her shoulder, gently grabbing Ellis's arm as if she's known her for years. I swear I see Ellis stiffen, but she quickly gets a hold of herself. That thrill of what we are doing runs through me again, my heart beating faster like I'm about to go cliff diving. "I don't think I've met you guys yet," Cass continues. Her eyes cut to me. "I'm the bride's cousin."

My mouth opens to answer, trying to intercept the conversation, but Ellis beats me to it. If the woman's presence had her stumbling before, there's no indication now.

"Ellie," she says, her voice casual—betraying nothing. "Oh, and this is my husband, Stuart."

A wicked smirk dances on her lips, and I fight the urge to laugh in this poor woman's face.

Well played.

"Oh." Cass drags the word out like our names don't ring a bell.

And of course, they don't.

One of them is completely made up.

She tilts her head to the side. Her red-painted lips pull into a friendly smile, green eyes glittering with the hope of meeting new friends—or at least that's what I assume she's doing.

Some part of me worries that she's onto us, and her cousin sent her over to kick us out.

"I don't think I'm familiar. You two are here for–" Cass lingers on the last word, waiting for us to fill in with whatever answer she's seeking.

This time, I chime in first. "The groom," I say. "Ellie is a close friend. Known him forever. I think they met at a hostel in Kansas."

"A hostel?" Cass questions, her brows pinched together.

Ellis nudges me, and the touch sends a jolt up my arm. "He's kidding," she tosses out. "About the hostel in Kansas part."

This seems to appease our new best friend. Her smile widens and she glances around the room, clearly searching for someone to introduce us to.

I watch as Ellis runs her tongue along her cheek before lifting her glass up to take another drink of champagne. I watch her swallow and quickly look away when my blood heats–images from the dressing room flashing in my mind.

"My boyfriend should be around here somewhere," Cass says, leaning to look behind me. "We should sit together!" Cass smiles at us before looking in the other direction, clearly distracted. "I'm so glad Angie gave up on the seating chart thing. She's been so stressed about the wedding. You know how anxious she gets. I'm sure Luke has told you all about it since you're friends."

Cass touches Ellis's shoulder, and I discreetly nudge her with my elbow, waiting for Angie's cousin to look away again. When the opportunity presents itself, and Ellis is the only one gazing at me, I raise my brows and mouth the words *no seating chart.*

She cocks a brow just as Cass waves someone down from across the room.

"Chad!" she shouts, stepping around Ellis to get his attention. "Come here. I want to introduce you to someone."

Ellis leans in, lowering her voice to a whisper, and suddenly we're in our own little world. This entire day feels like that, and while I can't bring it up in front of these people, considering we are undercover, I desperately want to know if she's enjoying crashing the wedding or not.

"Watch your drink." Ellis's voice remains quiet. "With a name like Chad, don't hand him that thing for nothing."

A soft chuckle drags from my chest as I lean into her, desperate for more of–*something.* "So judgmental."

Ellis doesn't have time to respond. Before we know it, a very put-together man stroking his trimmed beard confronts us and sizes us up like he's picking out the next horse he's purchasing for the Kentucky Derby.

"Stuart," Cass says, nodding to me first. "And Ellie. Ellie, this is my boyfriend, Chad."

Chad sticks his hand out to me first, and I shake it, trying to pretend I do this all the time. Unfortunately, my job doesn't consist of making billion-dollar deals. It consists of a lot of tech, and listening to a ton of music. My suit suddenly feels too tight, but I don't let it bother me.

"Nice to meet you," Chad says, a charming smile splitting his face. He looks down at Ellis, his eyes almost predatory, before shaking her hand. "And nice to meet you." His tone is off–a little too intrigued, and I become suspicious of him and his intentions.

Cass holds her cheerful expression, but I don't miss the look in her eyes when he leans forward. Just a touch.

I clear my throat. "My wife is a good friend of the groom. Your beautiful girlfriend here was just telling us she's the bride's cousin."

Chad's gaze cuts to me briefly before his eyes sneak down to Ellis's left hand. She quickly hides it, wrapping her arm around my back and leaning into me. She holds her champagne glass in her other hand, but all I can feel is the warmth of her arm at my back. My entire body lights up like I'm some sort of teenager. I scramble, trying to figure out what to do, and settle on draping my arm around her shoulder, angling my glass so *Chad* can't see the truth.

It would be a shame to get caught in our lie this early.

Cass quickly interrupts, placing a pale hand on Chad's arm. "I was *just* telling them they should sit with us."

"That would be nice," Chad says, adjusting his tie before his eyes track someone else in the crowd. He nods once with a quiet, "Excuse me."

Cass offers an apologetic smile, but there's a sadness behind her eyes, and I wonder if Ellis notices too. "I am going to run to the restroom, but I'll try to find you two after. It's so nice to meet new friends!"

"We would love to sit with you and Chad," Ellis calls as we watch Cass retreat into the crowd, her red dress disappearing into a sea of people.

As soon as the coast is clear, I take my arm off Ellis's shoulder and turn to her. "No seating charts," I say with a wicked grin decorating my lips.

"Such luck!" Ellis glances around to make sure nobody is listening. "Did you see Chad look down at my finger? Could he have been more obvious? Honestly, I feel bad for Cass."

I shift uncomfortably. "Do you want to sit with someone else?" I ask.

Ellis shakes her head before grinning. "No, no. I can't wait to tell them all about Kansas, Stuart."

I laugh, a deep sound rumbling out before I bring my drink to my lips. "I'm not really a champagne guy," I admit.

"Then why are you drinking it?"

I shrug. "You like champagne. It's your birthday. I thought it's what we were doing."

Ellis looks down at her drink, throwing the entire thing back before grabbing mine, and I watch with wide eyes.

"Okay then," I say with a chuckle.

"Makes me feel better about stealing. So, Stuart," she starts. "I didn't want to ask because I didn't want to sound like an idiot. What the hell is an AV tech?"

My chest warms at the question, and I run a hand over my tie, hoping to smooth that feeling down. I don't want it to be obvious how much I like her. I don't even *know* her. "It's an audio and visual technician," I supply. "I operate audio consoles and the PA systems in the auditorium. Video playback at events. Interface when bands and outside acts come onto campus."

"And are you *passionate* about it," she asks, a clear dig at what I implied regarding her job earlier.

"No." My tone is flat. "Well, I like when bands and acts come in. However, the thing pays well. It gives me a little stability. It's my freelance stuff I enjoy." I pause, remembering the song I worked on most recently. "As long as people are sending me good shit." I clear my throat. "Shit, sorry. I shouldn't be cursing. This is a classy event."

She laughs. Depositing her empty glass on another passing tray. "I'm sure it's fine. So, you like the music stuff. Play anything?"

My mouth quirks up. "A few instruments." As shitty as it is to admit, Noah had a point. Women typically flock to anything that plays an instrument. And damn it if I don't want Ellis to flock to me—if only a little.

"Main one?"

"Piano."

A shy smirk passes on her lips as she looks down, turning away briefly.

"Enough about me. I have more questions for you, Birthday Girl."

Someone walks into the hall from the double doors, speaking until the crowd quiets down to call us back into the ballroom.

"Looks like it'll have to wait," she whispers. "It's showtime."

Ten

Ellis

I'm clinging to Griffin like he's my lifeline.

Sitting at a table surrounded by strangers who don't know we aren't supposed to be here has me leaning a little closer and taking more risks–like when I grabbed his hand on top of the table while he lied his face off about his outlandish proposal.

I think he said something about an airplane writing in the sky while we were in the Bahamas. None of those things make sense because he also told the entire table, including Cass and Chad, that he works as a barista in a small local coffee shop three days a week and spends the other two days volunteering at the animal shelter.

Apparently, I'm an entrepreneur with a very successful business selling protein bars made with flour derived from crickets. It's a significant protein source, and the hip rock-climbing gyms around the U.S. eat it up.

I'm rich.

He's a freeloader.

I pull the flute to my lips, thankful for the cold water. After two glasses of champagne, I decided it was time to stick with something more sobering and the amazing meal the couple so graciously provided. Griffin tossed some cash into one of the wedding gifts, so my guilt about stealing has mostly subsided. The food also helped in my stay sober mission. Which is good because I need to be of sound mind and body to remember the massive amount of bullshit we are spewing.

Cass tilts her head back and laughs at something Griffin said, which makes sense because the man's been charming the pants off the entire table, even the old couple that joined us. They're apparently long-time friends of Angie's parents.

"So, Ellis," Chad says, licking his lips from across the table. The scowl he's wearing would make an infant cry for sure. I shift in my seat uncomfortably, thankful when Griffin puts his arm around the back of my chair. We make a pretty convincing married couple. I assume that's easy to do when reality is being postponed until the near feature.

"Yeah?" I say, setting my glass down.

"As Cass said, I own a successful golf club near Boston. It's one of my many businesses."

Griffin leans in, and I can feel his hot breath on my neck, sending a shiver down my spine. "One of his many businesses," he mocks so low I'm the only one to hear him. I suppress a chuckle.

"Anyway," Chad's expression doesn't change. "I'm wondering about these protein bars. This thing is really as successful as you say?"

"Oh, definitely!" My moral compass does not exist at this point. "Multi-million dollar company. You know how things are with those outdoorsy places. You can always upcharge if the packaging looks natural and earthy." I wave a hand, leaning back in my chair and feeling Griffin's suit jacket brush my bare shoulders. I chase the contact, leaning further into him and shutting off the responsible part of my brain. It's the part of my brain that's usually running overtime–the one that would remind me I don't know him.

This has been the best birthday of my entire life, and it's not even over.

"Well, I'm interested in making a deal to sell these things," Chad explains. "I'd love to talk about it."

"Oh, she won't sell in golf clubs," Griffin chimes in, a wicked smile dancing on his lips.

Chad grunts a little, leaning forward in his seat with that scowl still plastered on his too-perfect face. I'm pretty sure the guy has a heavy dose of self-tanner on. I'm not sure what Cass sees in him. She's just an absolute doll, and he's horrible.

"Why not?" Chad asks.

Griffin takes a bite of salmon and swallows before talking. "My darling, Ellis, is firmly against golf. A true animal lover. With my time volunteering at the shelter, and her passion for birds, we make quite a match."

Cass chuckles–a light and airy sound as she puts down her fork. "What does that have to do with golf?"

Griffin gets very serious, and Connie and James, the old couple that joined us, lean forward to listen as well–as if everything Griffin says is completely captivating. I mean, it is captivating–even if it's all lies. "You know that stray golf balls take out hundreds of birds every year."

The table is silent.

We are certifiably insane.

Luckily, we don't have to explain because the DJ comes on over the speakers with a microphone in hand. "Next thing on the list is The Decades Dance! Angie and Luke ask that all couples participate in this one, so grab your partner and get on the floor."

Lights flash across the small dance floor, forcing starbursts and shapes to dance around the tiled floors. I can't stop smiling when Griffin turns to me, the green flecks in his eyes catching the dim lights away from the action. Small wrinkles form at the corners of his eyes when he leans closer. And when he does that, it's almost like it draws me in, too.

Whatever atmosphere surrounds Griffin, I want to be in it–floating above the ground like I'm untouchable–like the rules don't matter.

"Golf balls and birds?" I question, fighting the urge to laugh.

"Real dangerous stuff. Can't have you selling your protein bars in his club. It's absolutely riddled with controversy."

I let the laugh loose then—a sound that comes deep from the pit of my belly. I don't even have time to be embarrassed about it or the strange snorting noises that come with it.

"Let's dance," Griffin says. "We are fake-married, after all. I want to treat you right for your birthday. Birthdays are a big deal in my family. I'm taking my responsibility very seriously."

"Technically," I say, "my birthday isn't for another three days."

He stands up, offering me his hand anyway. I don't question it, just put my own fingers in his and allow him to help me up, gently guiding me to the floor.

He shifts to walk behind me with a gentle hand on my back. When he bends down, his breath ghosts over my shoulder and my stomach dips. "Maybe we should just finish the bucket list." His deep voice is low, rumbling over my skin. "What are you doing tomorrow?"

I tilt back a little, grinning so hard my face hurts. "Busy," I say. "On Sundays, I stand outside of the local golf club and protest. It's for the birds, of course."

Griffin takes my arm and gently spins me around when we make it onto the dance floor. Couples gather all around us as soft music begins to play. It's some instrumental piano song, and I can't help but remember that he said he plays. I'd love to hear him play some-time.

Maybe I don't have to go back to being boring, responsible Ellis. Maybe I can just let this all continue–continue being whatever I've become around him.

My breath catches when his palm finds my waist, and he pulls me closer, his other hand in mine–warm and inviting–like everything about him.

"Forget the birds," he demands. "With all my free time, I've invented a special bird armor that will protect your precious fowl."

I laugh, my mind empty of all worries. I rest my forehead on his chest near his shoulder when he starts swaying; the music surrounding us. Griffin presses his cheek against my hair, his grip tightening infinitesimally.

"Go on another adventure with me, Ellis," he murmurs. "I don't want to be strangers again."

Whoa.

I look up at him, lips parted, face warm. I know he didn't mean to, but the words settled over me, prompting a flutter in my stomach–like a million dragonflies taking flight over a gentle pond in the country.

I promised myself I wouldn't ask questions. I promised I would let go–if only for a moment.

I don't let the feeling scare me and decide to take it all in–enjoy the weight of his hand on my waist and the bubble we've created on the dance floor.

My mouth quirks up as the DJ asks couples who have been married for less than five years to leave the floor. "Maybe," I whisper.

Griffin gives me another one of his devastating smiles, and I suddenly feel like the luckiest human alive for being on the receiving end of it.

We dance in silence, his hand in mine as the bodies slowly thin out around us. The remaining ones are certainly older, and I spot Connie and James across the way.

"How long have we been married, Stuart?" I ask.

His eyes are sparkling when he grips my hand tighter. "Well, the DJ is on ten years and up, so we've been married for a while."

"I'm twenty-four," I confess. "We've been married since I was fourteen."

Griffin's nose wrinkles. "A little young. I was sixteen when we got married. Best decision of my life."

I let out a breathy chuckle. "We should probably stop dancing. It's getting suspicious. We don't even have children yet."

"That's okay," he says. "You're focusing on your career, and I support your strange cricket farming habits."

After he says it, he releases my waist, and I suddenly miss the touch.

This entire thing is crazy.

Insane.

Hopelessly *fun*.

As we walk toward our table, the night dragging on outside of the windows of the ballroom, we run into a tall man with mussed hair and the scent of champagne on his breath. His tie is loosened, his white button-up wrinkled with his sleeves pushed up to his elbows.

He stumbles closer, clearly drunk.

"Angie doesn't know you guys," he slurs, pointing our way as alcohol sloshes over the lip of the glass he's holding. "Luke doesn't either."

My stomach drops to the floor–right out of my butthole. Instantly, my palms become sweaty and the adrenaline pumps through my blood.

"Must be mistaken." Griffin grabs my hand, promptly walking toward the door as the song starts coming to a close. Two couples left on the dance floor and the DJ now listing off the last numbers.

"You know," the guy catches up to us, rounding on Griffin and stepping closer to dig his finger into Finn's chest. "I don't think I am." All of his words are running together, and he's swaying on his feet.

Definitely drunk.

Definitely angry.

"I know my sister's friends," he asserts.

Griffin smiles, taking a step back, and his hand grips mine tighter. He hasn't let it go, and for that I'm thankful. "Well shit," he says. "Looks like we've been caught."

Angie's brother turns red–like an angry, drunk tomato.

"Are you good in heels?" Griffin asks, keeping his eyes on the brother while slowly backing away–dragging me with him.

"I'm alright."

"Okay." He smiles at me, and my entire body lights up with the thrill of excitement. I almost know what he's about to say before he says it. "Let's run."

When we turn to sprint, I hear chairs tumbling and shocked gasps sounding around the room. Griffin and I run through the entry hall and push through the doors, finding ourselves in the cold, open air of the grounds surrounding The Overlook.

A laugh tears from my lips, and we pause, realizing the brother is slower than we thought. I rip off my shoes, grabbing them both in one hand before turning to see the hunter coming after us.

With that, we both take off, laughing and filling our lungs with the bitter December air.

I thank Mother Nature that it hasn't snowed yet, but regardless, I don't feel the cold as my feet pound on the asphalt. I hike my dress up to get better movement–trying to keep up with Griffin's long strides.

The brother is yelling at us, parking lot lights illuminating the surrounding area. We sprint down the hill past the cars in the lot and toward some trees; the brother becoming faster and angrier with every step. When I see the tall chain-link fence in front of us, I start to think we have a chance.

"You like climbing?" Griffin yells over the wind whipping past my ears.

"I do now!"

We are both still laughing when we get there, looking back once to see if we have enough time.

I grab the sides of the dress, mud caked on my feet, as Griffin takes my shoes from me. "Up you go," he says, and I squeeze my feet through the small holes in the fence. Somehow, this was much easier when I was a kid—less painful, too. Even so, with the threat of an angry brother on our tail, I start climbing.

It's not fast enough. I can hear the yelling behind us, and Griffin reaches up, pushing a hand on my butt and giving me a shove until I can grab the top of the fence, struggling with the skirt of my dress and trying to figure out how I will hurl one leg over. Finn's hand is still firmly on my ass.

"You're really feeling me up," I say. Griffin removes his hand instantly, and I hear the fence rattle as he climbs next to me.

We are both winded and focused.

"These are not the circumstances in which I imagined palming your ass," he responds, and my foot slips. Quickly regaining my composure, I risk another glance back and haul my very felt-up ass higher.

I throw my leg over the top and hear the rip cut through my thrifted dress. The cold night air hits my thigh, but I refuse to look down at the dress when the ground sits further below me. Hopefully, I've just created a nice and tasteful slit.

Behind us, I can see the brother has given up, standing higher on the hill and waving us off as he turns around. Griffin tosses his leg over, and before I know it, we are both in the grass, safe and cold—caked in dirt and sweat.

I'm panting, my hands on my knees as I look through the fence chains and up the empty hill. When I stand up straight, my gaze slides to Griffin, sitting in the mud-mixed grass with his legs stretched out and his hands resting behind him. He's staring up at the sky, his chest heaving as he tries to get his breathing under control.

"You imagined palming my ass?" I ask, placing my hands on my hips.

His eyes snap to mine, and I swear I see a slight tint to his cheeks in the small amount of light meeting us from the parking lot. "I didn't mean to say that." He clears his throat. "Fuck, Ellis. I'm sorry."

I chuckle, moving to stand in front of him. When I offer him my hand, he takes it easily, standing up to his full height and towering above me. The smile is gone, and I can tell he suddenly feels uncomfortable.

"It's really okay," I assure. "Absolutely fine."

A breathy laugh escapes him as he looks at the ground, shoving his hands in his pocket. The expression makes him look younger–vulnerable. "You still want to hang out? There's something else I think we can check off the list tonight."

I take one more deep breath, finally coming down from the high of our impromptu marathon. "Yeah?" I realize I left my phone in his car and try not to think about how reckless that was. "What time is it?"

He grabs his from his pocket to check, the gentle glow illuminating his face. "Eleven-thirty. I know it's really late, but I'm fine if you want to–"

"Yes!" I say, and he meets my smile with his own. "But before we leave, I feel like I should confess that I lied to you about something."

"Ellis." He rolls his eyes. "We lied about nearly everything tonight."

I don't let his comment derail me. "I don't park far away because I'm afraid people will hurt my car. Which I need to pick up, by the way."

His smile drops, and his brows furrow. It's the cutest thing I've ever seen. "Okay?"

"I park far away because I'm a bad driver, and parking between two cars gives me anxiety."

Griffin shakes his head, the smile returning to his lips as he pulls off his suit jacket and offers it to me. "Alright," he says. "You're forgiven. Now let's go before our adrenaline runs out, and we start to remember it's winter."

Eleven

Griffin

I lean back, resting my head on the seat in my car as I stare out toward my apartment building. I dropped Ellis off near the thrift store to pick up her vehicle. When I look at the clock on my dashboard and read *one a.m.,* I start to think that maybe she's gone home.

Did she get home safely?

I should have gotten her number or at least given her mine.

Pulling out my phone, I glance at my text messages and see a thread from Noah.

Noah: *I need an update.*
Noah: *How was Angie's wedding?*
Noah: *You still with her?*

I stare at the screen, my eyes heavy as I think up a response.

Me: *Got chased out of the wedding. It was fun. She's supposed to meet me at my place soon.*

I wince, reading the message over again and realizing what Noah might infer. I quickly type out clarification to keep him from drawing conclusions.

Me: *Not what you think.*

I watch the typing bubble appear, and moments later, a giant eggplant emoji shows up on my screen.

I roll my eyes and shove my phone back in my pocket, looking up just in time to see the headlights shine into my windows, a car driving slowly around the parking lot.

In the dark, I can't see what the car looks like, so pull the door handle and crawl out of the Jeep. If it's not Ellis, then I tell myself I should give up–go inside and move on.

Luckily, I watch as the car pulls around and parks a few spaces down. Ellis sits in the driver's seat and puts the car in park. She cuts the engine and climbs out with the corduroy button down over her ripped and muddied dress.

She smiles, pulling a backpack over her shoulder before meeting me on the sidewalk in front of my place.

"Hey." My hands are in my pockets, the icy wind kissing my cheeks as the dark sky stretches overhead. Half of her face is shadowed, the streetlight illuminating the other half.

"Hey." Ellis wraps her arms around herself to fight off the cold. "Ready to write the next pop hit?"

I chuckle, my breath billowing out in front of my face. The December air swirls around us and I nod toward the steps. "Third floor," I say, "And absolutely."

We climb the steps in silence, and I can almost hear my heart pounding in my chest. It's hard to know how to behave around her. On one hand, we are complete strangers, but on the other, we just spent the last four hours pretending to be a married couple at a wedding we weren't even invited to. Now that we're alone, there's more distance between us.

"This is it." I fish my apartment key out of my pocket and unlock the door to invite her in.

Ellis steps in behind me and immediately looks around the dark before carefully closing the door. I can't see her expression until I walk through the living room to flick on the lamp. The light shines over the breakfast nook, the galley kitchen, and the living space in one go.

"It's not a very big apartment," I admit, suddenly aware of how bare my walls are and the plate and cup still sitting on the black coffee table. I quickly pick them up and deposit them into the sink.

"It's nice," she says, "but I don't see a piano."

"It's a keyboard, technically, and it's in the closet."

Her eyes widen, and I notice the way she cracks her knuckles, wondering how nervous she must be showing up here–thankful that she did.

"The apartments here are small, but they have decent sized walk-in closets as part of the master bedroom." I clear my throat, suddenly aware of how that sounds. "It's where I keep all my music stuff. I won't bore you with the details, but it's less work to treat the room when it's smaller. It is, however, large enough to hold a bunch of my shit."

She nods, eyes flicking to the breakfast nook in the corner.

"Here," I say, taking a step back to give her space. "I'm going to go change. I have some clothes in the guest bedroom since my closet is currently being used. You can go back there first, check it out. If you're nervous, I'd be happy to give you a kitchen knife." My mouth quirks up at one corner. "If for any reason you feel unsafe, you're welcome to stab me with it."

She laughs then, her shoulders relaxing, and I'm thankful for it. It's a glimpse of the version of Ellis I saw at the wedding–one more puzzle piece to place.

"I don't need a knife, but I do need to change. This dress is disgusting and ripped." She pulls the backpack from her shoulder. "I brought my other outfit."

My eyes flick to the tan bag, remembering how she looked in the coffee shop. The turtleneck, the jeans. "Do you want something else to wear?" Her eyes widen at that, and I quickly clear my throat.

"You don't have to. I just meant if you wanted something more comfortable."

"You just keep women's clothes on hand for–" Ellis lingers on the last word, waiting for me to finish the thought as she tucks a black strand of hair behind her ear.

"I meant one of my T-shirts." She nods again, a soft smile gracing her lips. "Maybe a pair of basketball shorts or something. I didn't want you to be uncomfortable is all, and I don't have many women over."

I start fumbling over my words. "Not that I have never had women over. I'm not weird."

Ellis snorts, considering my offer as her eyes fix to the black leather couch in the living room. When her gaze finally meets mine, I settle a bit at her expression.

"That would be nice," she says.

I turn to walk down the hall, muttering that I'll be back before leaving her in my living room and hoping she will still be there when I emerge. I dig through the closet in my guest bedroom, finding two T-shirts, and some athletic shorts.

Ellis is standing by the end table near the couch, running a finger along the frame of an old photograph of my family. I had to have been about thirteen in the picture. My parents, my sister Skylar, my brother–we're all there, smiling.

Ellis startles when she notices me looming behind her, and I really hope she isn't re-evaluating my serial killer status. She quickly hides her hands behind her back as if I caught her doing something wrong.

"Sorry," she says. "I was just looking. Trying to make sure you still aren't Ted Bundy."

I laugh, handing her the clothes and giving her directions to the bathroom before disappearing to change out of my suit.

My button-down has mud streaked across the chest, and my pants are covered in dirt and sweat. I wince as I peel the clothes off my body in the guest bedroom, throwing them in a hamper and replacing them with a T-shirt and basketball shorts. I throw a gray hoodie over my head and quickly push up the sleeves before returning to the hallway.

My mind is a swirl of everything that's happened in the past eight hours. The coffee shop, pretending to be married, and making up outrageous lies about who we were. All of those memories settle in, making their way into the box marked *the most fun* in the back of my mind. When I accepted the freelance job from some girl who spilled her coffee on her head, I couldn't have known this is how it would go.

Now that we are away from the wedding, it's a little harder to know what's expected of me. It certainly has nothing to do with Noah's eggplant emoji.

The nerves swirl in my gut, reminding me she's no longer hanging out with *Stuart*. She's about to hang out with Griffin, and I really want her to fucking like that.

I stand outside the bathroom door, knuckles raised, but before I can knock, Ellis is standing there with a shirt halfway down her thighs, and basketball shorts to her knees. Her hands clasp the sides of them when she looks up at me and steps back, startled. "Oh, hey."

I put my hands up in defense. "I was just about to knock, I swear."

She tilts her head to the side, humor dancing in her gaze. "You don't make a habit of lingering outside of bathrooms and waiting for women to emerge with your clothes on?"

I chuckle, my face warming with embarrassment. "No."

Ellis offers me a wide smile, white teeth flashing before looking down at her outfit. "The shorts are big," she says. "We should find somewhere to sit down so they don't fall off." Her eyes lift infinitesimally, lingering on my thigh just beneath my shorts. "Nice tattoos." I watch her eyes flick to the ones on my arms, the patchwork of different stories I've tried to document–memories. Some good and some–memorable.

"Thanks." I look down the hallway toward my room. "Well, our song isn't going to write itself." I turn on my heel, socks shuffling on the carpet as I lead her to the giant walk-in closet that sold this entire apartment to me.

I flick on the dim lamp in the corner next to a beanbag, and gesture for her to sit there. Unfortunately, since this is a literal closet, I don't have space for proper seating–something I hadn't worried about until right this second.

I walk over to the stool in front of my makeshift desk decorated with a computer screen, outboard gear, nearfield monitors, a random granola bar wrapper.

Quickly grabbing the trash and throwing it in the bin behind my setup, I sit down, spinning in my chair until I see Ellis sprawled on top of the bean bag, her eyes closed as she tips her head back, and I'm suddenly aware of two things. One, it's very late, and two, there's a beautiful woman sitting in my closet wearing my clothes. My entire body blazes like the sun and my cheeks are red. I just fucking know it.

When I turn around to face my keyboard, I flick it on, hearing Ellis's voice from the corner.

"I can't believe we just met, and I get to hear you play. Usually, people pretend it's some giant secret—like exposing the deepest parts of them. Very dramatic stuff. Very intimate."

Please don't say that.

"It's not intimate." I tap a few keys, glancing at the bass traps decorating the walls. "I like playing for people."

"Okay, so play me something."

I spin on the stool, seeing her with her head propped up in her hand. Her hair spills over her shoulders in waves, that wide smile splitting her face.

"Aren't we supposed to be writing a song for your birthday?" I ask, my own smile dancing at the edge of my lips as I lean down to rest my elbows on my knees and clasp my hands in front of me.

"It's late, and I need to be inspired." She looks comfortable, and I can't help but take it as a win. "I want to feel like my entire world has changed when I listen to you play. Just like every other girl you've taken into your little thirst trap music den."

My low laugh sneaks out of me. "Thirst trap?" I question.

Her cheeks flush, and she looks away. "Sorry," she mumbles. "It was a joke. I thought it would be funny." Ellis places her hands in her lap, watching as she picks at her nails. "I'm not usually this comfortable around strangers, but we have been married for over ten years, so I guess that changes things." A breathy laugh escapes her lips, and her eyes meet mine–darker in the dim lighting. It's like there's a depth there just waiting to be discovered. "I didn't mean any of that. I just want to hear you play."

I run a hand over my dark hair, keeping one elbow placed on my knee as I look up at her. "It was funny, however inaccurate. I don't use this place as a thirst trap, though Noah would disagree."

"Noah?" she questions.

"One of my friends." I turn on the stool, tap a few notes and test out the keyboard again. "English professor who works at the college where I work. Young, newly subscribed to a dark academia aesthetic. If anything, he's the walking thirst trap. I'm sure he has read every Jane Austen novel just so he can charm the pants off intellectual women everywhere."

Ellis snorts, propping her head in her hand again and messing with the hem of my basketball shorts she's wearing. "Kind of brutal to your friend."

"Nah," I say, thinking about the singular emoji message I left on read earlier. "He's brutal to me. Plus, his mom and my mom are friends."

"They both set up your playdates?"

My tongue rolls along my cheek as I suppress a smile. "Sometimes."

Ellis's gaze flicks down, landing on the tattoo on my forearm and my smile drops, nerves suddenly pulsing through my blood as she analyzes me. I suppose if I were in her situation, I'd be trying to figure me out, too.

"What's that one for?" she asks, and I look down at my arm.

"Which one?"

"The tattoo of the vintage car. The beetle, with all the flowers growing out of it. I like it. It's pretty." Ellis plays with the ends of her hair. "What is it for?"

I clear my throat, wondering how she picked that particular tattoo out of all of them. I run a finger over the car, remembering when I got it. "It's for my brother," I offer. "Died in a car accident when I was sixteen." A heaviness drops over the room, and I hate the way it makes me feel—the way it reminds me of how everyone responded to my entire family right after the crash. I long to get rid of the weight of it.

"That's—" She doesn't look at me with pity, just blinks and looks at the tattoo briefly before meeting my gaze. "It's cool. I like it."

I chuckle. "My brother dying?"

"The tattoo, you idiot."

I place my hand on my heart, acting injured. "Ouch. Kick a man while he's down." I rub the spot, and she laughs, stretching her legs out from where she sits in the beanbag.

"I lost my mom when I was thirteen," she confesses, her smile dropping. "Breast cancer. My aunt raised me."

"And she's not around for your birthday?" I ask, my brow quirking up. I'm anxious for more information about her life—more pieces of truth instead of her fake job selling cricket protein bars.

"She was young. Twenty-four and fresh out of college when I descended on her life unintentionally. She's on a cruise with her family this week." Ellis offers a small smile, one that says she doesn't mind—like she's glad. "B deserves it. She's done a lot for me." She shifts on the beanbag before clearing her throat and looking at me again, brown eyes boring into my own.

When I asked her to come back to write a song, this isn't exactly what I had in mind, but something about the late hour makes people a little more vulnerable—more honest.

"And your dad?" I ask.

Her nose scrunches before she responds. "More of a ghost than my mom." She shrugs. "I don't know him. I suppose he's out there somewhere, but considering I've never met him, I imagine he's rather unpleasant. Eventually, I stopped thinking about him. No use in hurting my own feelings." One corner of her mouth pulls up, the heavy weight still bearing down on the room.

"So, a car accident?" she asks, and I can't help but feel she's trying to draw attention away from what she just said. My chest aches, but I know how that kind of sympathy can feel, so I stuff it down and don't ask her for more.

"Yeah." I grab the hood of my sweatshirt and pull it over my head. "Nothing crazy. It was raining, and he hydroplaned."

It's quiet in the room—a moment of pause before Ellis speaks again. "That sucks."

I turn on the stool, tapping a few more keys to fill the silence. "Honestly?" I look down at the tattoo one more time, wondering what she might pull out of me if she asks about the others. Of course, she picked the heaviest one first. Some of them are absolute bullshit—just messing around with friends. My gaze slides in her direction. "I was more concerned about hiding his weird, fucking anime porn from my mom when it happened."

The cackle she releases breaks the weird heaviness in the room, and for that, I'm thankful.

"So, what song are you thinking about writing?" I ask. "It's your bucket list, after all. Should we rewrite the lyrics to *Happy Birthday*?"

She laughs again. "Oh, come on Finn. We can do better than that."

Ellis stands up, hovering over me as she taps a few keys on her own, the notes playing in the room as she raises a brow. "Let's write a cheesy wedding song for our dear friends, Angie and Luke." She taps another key, and my eyes track the movement before meeting her gaze once more. Her scent invades my lungs. She smells like fresh flowers in spring, and I decide that I've found the cure for seasonal depression.

It's Ellis.

Something spikes in my blood, but I keep it contained. "It's only right," I offer.

She nods once, a false seriousness overtaking her expression. "After stealing their champagne? You're absolutely correct."

Twelve

Ellis

The only thing scarier than crashing a wedding with a complete stranger was having a fancy-looking microphone shoved in my face and being expected to repeat whatever madness we had crafted in the forty-five minutes we spent writing our song.

Finn started out with the keyboard, pressing a few keys and slowly working into something that sounded like real music. I had sat listening to him play, and while I didn't want to admit that I had some of those feelings I joked about, I did.

Slowly, the song transformed into something else, and a melody broke through–the lyrics following. And while I'd never written a song before, I would be lying if I said I didn't think it was good.

I click the lock button on my phone, glancing at the floor where it sits next to the beanbag and reading four a.m. on the screen. Sometime after I finished singing my heart out, somewhat hesitant at first, I walked back into the other room to grab my backpack and fished out my sketchbook and charcoal pencils–everything I needed to pass the time while Griffin picked up different instruments, working quietly as he pieced together this *thing* we had created together.

I look at the sketch, brushing away stray eraser pieces. I had drawn Finn, sitting on his stool with a water bottle on the floor, the sleeves of his sweatshirt pulled down, and his hood up with headphones on as he stared at a monitor.

Griffin pulls one side of the headphones back so he can hear and turns on the stool, swiveling in my direction. "You've been working on that for a while," he states. "What are you drawing?"

"Ha." I snap the sketchbook shut. "Top secret stuff. Spy work, actually. I lied about my job."

His eyes sparkle in the dim light of the lamp, and I wonder how we are both still awake. "I knew it." He pulls the headphones off fully, wrapping them around the back of his neck. "You aren't passionate about marketing."

I tilt my head to the side and shrug. "Guilty." Placing the sketchbook and pencil on the floor near my feet, I look up again. "How much longer until we have a real-life song?"

"A few more hours." He swivels back and forth on the chair, stretching his arms up before pulling his hood down and placing his hands on the back of his head. A small sliver of skin flashes above his basketball shorts, and I glance away. That little sliver of stomach is kryptonite to all women everywhere. Especially when it's Griffin's.

"It has to be perfect," he finishes.

I clear my throat, fighting the insecurity that rises in me. "My voice is that bad, huh?"

To throw him off my scent and make him believe I'm *not* nervous about the whole singing thing, I offer him a casual smile.

"Not your voice." His smirk tells me everything I need to know as he sways back and forth on the stool. His eyes linger on me and my heart beats like a kick drum–keeping time with the music we've created.

My phone vibrates from the floor, and I watch as Lennon's name pops up for a Facetime call.

"Do you care if I answer this?" I ask.

"Go ahead."

When I click the green button, her face fills the screen, red hair piled in a messy bun on her head. "I was just getting up to let my parents' dog out," she says by way of greeting. "You never texted me at all! Are you alive, bitch?" Her brows furrow, the pause loaded with tons of realization. "Wait." Lennon's eyes widen. "Whose shirt is that? Where are you? Oh my god, Ellie!"

I shush her as Finn's deep chuckle sounds from where he's still sitting. He puts his headphones back on, and turns toward the monitor, giving us privacy, I suppose.

"You're still with him!"

"Hello, Lennon. How are you? Are you enjoying Minnesota? Did your mom recover from her food poisoning?"

"Fuck my mother!" Lennon stands up, carrying the phone with her across the room until she pauses and I hear a sliding door open followed by dog nails clicking on the hardwood. "Respectfully," she adds. "Spill everything. Can he still hear me?"

I glance up at Griffin, wondering the same thing. He doesn't seem to be listening. "Finn?" I say. No response. He's clicking around on the monitor, doing whatever it is he's supposed to be doing to craft the music industry's next greatest hit.

"I don't think so." I flip the camera around, revealing Finn in his sweatshirt with his headphones on and his thigh tattoos on full display below his shorts. I don't want to admit what those do to me. They're woefully slutty.

"He's fucking hot, Ellie!"

I giggle.

Like a schoolgirl.

"I know," I whisper, leaning over to grab my own water bottle from the floor, carefully trying to unscrew the cap with one hand to take a drink. I manage the task successfully, and when I set it back down, I see the feral smile on Lennon's face.

"Did you–"

My stomach drops. "No!" I interrupt before she can finish, the heat of a million wildfires rushing to my face. "But I *do* have to go."

"Are you going to–"

I roll my eyes. "No, Lennon. Not tonight."

She wiggles her brows. "Not tonight? Okay, okay. Well, I have to go anyway, too. My parents are probably going to wake up from all my screeching." She's walking up a set of stairs in a dark hallway. "Call me tomorrow?"

"Sure."

Lennon hangs up, and the cracked door to Finn's closet opens a bit more, creaking as a black, fluffy creature prowls into the room.

Finn turns around, taking his headphones off again. "Simon," he offers. "He doesn't usually like strangers. He's probably been hiding, but I suppose he got curious."

"I almost forgot you said you had a cat." The cat walks over to me, and I reach my hand down, letting him sniff me before he rubs his face on my fingers and lets me pet under his chin. My heart is suddenly warm and fuzzy and about to explode. "He's cute."

Finn bites the inside of his cheek, suppressing a smile as he stares at me, and my brows furrow.

"What?" I say.

"Nothing."

"No, tell me."

"You think I'm fucking hot?"

My face is in my hands faster than Christian inviting a stranger to coffee. The embarrassment has me wanting to crawl into the Earth to move as far away from Finn as possible. "Oh my god," I mutter.

"It's fine," he says. "Payback for the ass comment earlier."

I can't look at him. I slowly pick up my sketchbook and wish some freak accident would just take me out. End my life so I don't have to see his *fucking hot* face again.

"So, you've been drawing in that, right?" I risk a glance upward, noting that there's no judgment there. I'm thankful for that. "Drawing for your fancy spy job, of course."

I sigh. "Yeah." Opening the sketchbook, I flip to a page with a park scene–anything but my sketch of Finn.

He stands up, moving closer and sitting himself on the floor next to the beanbag. When he takes the book, my heart pounds rapidly in my chest. He's flipping through it, and I'm nervous he's going to see the image I drew of him.

"These are really good," he says. "I'm not sure why you'd pick marketing if you can do all this." He turns the sketchbook on its side, looking at one of the drawings I did of Lennon. She practically commissioned it–for free, of course.

"Well, you know," I say. "Art isn't exactly stable."

"I get it. That's why I have the AV tech job." He hands the book back to me, and I shove it in my bag, thankful he didn't find the sketch of himself and see how freaking weird I am. "My mom paints," he continues. "She's actually very good. Her stuff sometimes ends up in local art shows. I'm sure she'd love to see those."

I chuckle and look away. Not wanting to linger on the fact that he just said I should show his sketches to his mother.

Like, meet his mom.

"That's really cool." I'm not sure how to respond. The late hour starts to weigh on me, making my bones feel tired, and I think about driving home–or falling asleep right here. The latter is probably the safer option.

When I turn, Finn's gaze fixes on mine. There's no smile on his face, only a strange heat in his eyes that makes my stomach dip and swirl, catching me off guard. I can't look away.

Without thinking, my lips part, and Finn reaches up slowly, like he's debating what he's doing the entire time he's doing it. A warm finger tucks a strand of hair behind my ear, and my breath catches, our eyes still locked into whatever moment this is.

I should definitely go to bed. My moral compass is worse than it was at the wedding. I'm not thinking clearly, and I'm having all sorts of weird thoughts about what Lennon implied earlier.

Those long fingers remain tangled in the strands of my hair. The fingers that just played music–crafted something beautiful from nothing. With my heart pounding in my ears, I try to think clearly.

"I'm tired," I announce, breaking some of whatever tension was stretching between us.

Finn clears his throat, pulling away and leaning back against the wall. There's a soft smile on his lips, and if he feels awkward about what just happened, he doesn't show it. "You can stay here if you want." He shakes his head a little, running his fingers through his hair. He looks nervous–the only sign of what just happened. "In the guest bedroom," he clarifies.

Simon stretches out on the carpet in front of us before laying down and rolling over to expose his belly.

"That would be nice."

Finn gets out his phone, scrolling until he stops and reads something there. He types a quick message and pockets the device before speaking. "Do you want to get a tattoo tomorrow?"

"What?"

"It's on the bucket list, and I know a guy." He gestures to himself. "Clearly. I'm sure he could squeeze us in. We're good friends."

A smile splits my face, the idea sending a thrill through my blood. "That would be so fun."

Finn stands up and offers me his hand.

I take it, standing and stretching to ward off some of my exhaustion. My eyelids start to feel heavy, and I begin to wonder if staying awake until four a.m. is the stuff of the past. I'm probably getting too old for this. "Are you sure you want to keep hanging out?" I ask, planting myself in front of him as he looks down at me. Something in his eyes tells me the answer before it even passes through his lips.

"Absolutely," he says. "I kind of want to get a new tattoo, anyway. It'll be fun."

I chuckle then, toying with the fabric of his basketball shorts that I'm still wearing. "We just officially met like eleven hours ago, and we are going to get tattoos together?"

His smile widens, something flashing behind his hazel eyes. "Actually," he says. "I have a better idea."

"What?"

"We can still get you your tattoo, but I bet Ryan would let you use his gun."

My brow furrows as I try to follow his train of thought. "What do you mean?" I ask.

Finn clears his throat again. "I saw your sketches, Ellis." He runs his hand through his hair. A nervous tick, and I watch the tendons in his arms flex. "Why don't you give me a tattoo?"

"Me?" I practically shriek the word, eyes wide as I try to figure out if he's serious.

"Sure," he says. "I already have plenty. What's one more? It'll be fun."

I eye him suspiciously. "You're not giving me my tattoo, are you?"

Finn chuckles and turns toward the door, opening it to reveal his bedroom beyond. I try not to focus on that detail too much—especially now that he knows I find him attractive, and I know that he's thought about palming my ass.

"Absolutely not," he says. "I'll leave that to the professionals."

I follow him out the door, and we walk through the bedroom to the hallway, Simon on our heels. "You're sure you trust me enough for that?" I ask when he leads me to the guest bedroom, opening the door and waiting.

"What do you mean?" he says. "We've been married for ten years, Ellis." I laugh at that. "Of course, I trust you."

We stand in the hallway, smiling like idiots as I think about the thrill of tomorrow—the new adventure we are about to go on. If he seriously lets me give him a tattoo, it will single-handedly be the best moment of my natural life. I've loved drawing for as long as I can remember, and he liked my sketches enough to trust me to do this.

I'm giddy.

And sleepy.

He must see it, too.

"Goodnight, Ellie," he murmurs, and I don't miss the way he uses my nickname. It warms something in my chest, and I realize he must have heard it during my conversation with Lennon.

I nervously play with the hem of his T-shirt. "Goodnight, Finn," I say.

Griffin turns, walking back to his door at the end of the hall. Before he disappears, he looks back once, the smile still painted on his lips, and I can't help the way my entire body lights up. I move into his guest bedroom, noting the made-up bed with the floral quilt stretched out over the top. I make a note to ask him about the quilt tomorrow.

What man has a floral quilt in their guest bedroom?

When I crawl under the covers, I feel the excitement of the day turn to exhaustion and burrow deep into my body, reminding me I probably should have been sleeping hours ago.

As soon as I close my eyes, sleep takes me, and I dream of tattoos and weddings.

Thirteen

Griffin

The sunlight floats through my window—tinted gray from the overcast winter sky.

I stretch out on my stomach, my sweatshirt and T-shirt deposited on top of the dresser in the corner, reminding me of the night before.

Ellis is still in my apartment

At least I hope she is.

I snatch my phone off the nightstand and glance at the time to read *ten a.m.* before opening up my text messages. Ryan's name pops up, and I'm seriously hoping what I said to Ellis will be the truth—that he can squeeze us in for tattoos today.

Ryan: *Why the fuck were you texting me at four-thirty?*
Ryan: *I have an hour from eleven to noon. As long as it's nothing crazy, it should be fine.*

I smile at that, rolling onto my back to type a response.

Me: *We'll be there if it's still open*
Ryan: *You got it*

A loud crashing sound echoes from the kitchen, and my smile widens. At least she didn't leave.

I quickly roll out of bed, glimpsing Simon sitting perched on the windowsill–ruining my fucking blinds again.

I snatch my T-shirt off the dresser and nod toward the door like the cat can understand me.

"Come on, let's get you a late breakfast. I'm sure your bowl is empty."

Simon leaps from the window, prancing into the hallway as I trail after him, following the sounds of dishes clinking and the sink running.

When I round the corner to the entrance of the galley kitchen, I see Ellis standing in my shirt and shorts, her black hair frizzy and uncombed. She grips an empty coffee cup, clearly in the middle of helping herself.

And for some reason, I like that. *A lot.*

"Hey," I say softly, and she startles. Jumping and spinning so fast that I can't help but laugh.

"Jesus," she yelps.

Her eyes flick down to my chest, and I quickly pull the T-shirt on over my head to cover up. While I don't mind her looking, I'm also quick to consider that waking up in a man's apartment when you've known him for less than twenty-four hours might not be a typical thing for her. In fact, I get the very real impression that most of what we did has never been a thing for her, and I desperately want her to feel comfortable here–around me.

She clearly shut things down last night when I was sitting on the floor next to her and thinking about kissing her.

Got to rein it in.

"Helping yourself to coffee?" I ask, and Ellis slumps, leaning against the counter.

"I feel half-alive," she admits.

I gesture toward the coffeepot before turning around and grabbing the grounds out of the cabinet. "Then, by all means," I reply. I set the bag next to her. "We can't have you dying on my watch. Ryan said we are good for tattoos, but we will have to leave in forty minutes. I don't feel right about tattooing a dead person."

She stands up straight, eyes swimming with a question. "Can I shower?"

A crooked smile appears on my face. "Sure. You may smell like Old Spice, though."

"That's fine." She looks down at the coffee pot still in her hand, wondering what to do with it exactly.

I reach out and take it from her, our fingers brushing briefly and sending a jolt of energy through my veins. I try not to acknowledge it.

"Here," I say, moving to the sink and running the water. "Let *me* make this for you. You go get ready."

She scurries off down the hallway, and I find myself wondering what tattoo she might get.

Simon weaves himself between my legs to remind me of my fatherly duties. I grab his food from under the sink, using the child lock for the cabinet because the creature is smarter than he looks.

After feeding Simon and pouring a cup of coffee, I anxiously set out every option for creamer I have in my fridge. I also grab sugar and honey and two different-sized spoons before making my way back to the bedroom. Digging out a pair of jeans, a clean black T-shirt, and a black hoodie, I can't help the smile that creeps onto my face.

• • • ● • ● • ● • •

"Have you decided what you're getting?"

Ellis walks beside me wearing the clothes she wore to the coffee shop yesterday, her Converse tapping the damp street where it must have rained last night.

I can't wait for it to actually snow. The Midwest is ugly during the in-between.

I open the door to the tattoo shop, gesturing for her to go in ahead of me.

"No clue," she tosses over her shoulder, "but I have a few ideas floating around in my head. I'm sure I'll settle on one of them at the last minute."

"You mean to tell me you've had this on your bucket list and you've never once thought about what you'd get?" I raise my brows at her, and she glances around the shop, taking in the strange art hanging on the walls, the glass windows toward the entrance, and the wooden bench sitting next to the smallest glass case I've ever seen filled with miscellaneous body jewelry.

"It's a lot of pressure, okay?"

Ryan appears from around the corner, his gold nose ring catching the light as he runs his hand over his cropped hair. His T-shirt reveals the sleeve of tattoos running up his arm, decorating his brown skin with images of a compass, a pirate ship, and a moon reflecting off water.

"Hey, Griffin," he says, walking around the desk and grabbing my hand, bringing me in, and patting my back once before letting go.

"Still good for tattoos?" I ask, smiling as Ryan's eyes flick from me to Ellis.

"Yeah. Just you or–" Ryan's brows furrow. "Oh, sorry. I should introduce myself. I'm Ryan."

He holds out his hand, and Ellis takes it. "Ellis," she says. "Finn's friend."

His full lips break into a wide smile. "Finn?" he questions. I shake my head, staring at the wooden floors beneath my tennis shoes. I'm so bent out of shape for this girl, and I barely know her. As soon as

Ryan gets me alone, I'm going to receive so much shit. All the shit. It'll be like a cattle farm.

"She's getting her first tattoo," I offer, looking back up at Ryan.

"Oh, sweet! What are you getting? Hopefully, I'll have time to get it all done for you. If not, you can always schedule an appointment. Any girl who's a friend of Griffin's gets priority. He doesn't bring girls around much." Ryan nudges her arm and Ellis laughs.

"Um–" she considers for a moment before snatching my arm from me and pushing up my sleeve to show the tattoo I have for my brother. Ellis looks at me. "What flowers are these?" she asks.

I look at my arm where she's still holding me, her hands cold against my skin but somehow making my entire body warm, anyway. "Some lily of the valley, baby's breath, daisies," I list out.

"I want those," she says, her eyes catching mine briefly before she turns to Ryan. "I want the same flowers," she says.

"Do they have some kind of meaning?" Ryan asks with a chuckle, and I can't imagine how weird it looks that Ellis just decided to get the same flowers tattooed on her body.

"I'm going to get them for my mom," she answers.

My heart stutters. I'm not sure what to think as my eyes slide toward her, staring at the side of her face and taking in the wide smile she's wearing. Her shoulders are relaxed, her body casual, as if she didn't just agree to get a near-matching tattoo to memorialize her dead mother. The same tattoo I have to memorialize my dead brother.

"Anything aside from the flowers?" Ryan asks. "Do you want them in something? Maybe some script with them?"

I'm still staring at her and blinking, my stomach doing weird turns and twists as I try to wrap my mind around this fucking girl.

Twenty-four hours ago, she was just some girl I watched spill coffee on her head who wanted a stranger to plan her birthday party.

And now it feels like, I don't know, more? Friends?

"I haven't had a ton of time to think about all this," she says. "I think Finn's tattoo is sweet. Maybe mine can be on a vintage bike or something? Back of my arm above my elbow?"

Ryan looks at me again, giving me a knowing look—as if he suspects something is going on between me and the girl I brought into his shop.

He doesn't know the half of it.

"I'll sketch something up and be right back," he says as another customer emerges from the door.

When he's gone, I turn to Ellis. "You're sure about this?" I ask, and I can't help the way my throat clogs with emotion. I will not do something fucking stupid like tearing up in this tattoo shop over flowers and dead people.

Ellis shrugs. "Yeah. I like yours, and it seems like something I won't regret in the morning. Dead mom and all. It's not like she's coming back."

I suppress a laugh. "I forgot to ask him about mine."

"Oh, yes." The smile dances on her lips. "What do you want to get? Please keep it simple. I'm new to this."

"Surprise me," I say. "I like my tattoos to bring up memories, and I think that maybe I'd like it if I remembered our time together." I clear my throat, nervously running my hand through my hair and pulling at the dark strands briefly. "I'd like to remember you, Ellis." Her eyes light up from where she's standing, and I suck in a breath, telling myself to be brave. "I'd like to keep not being strangers, too. If that's okay with you."

Ellie tilts her head, her finger brushing against mine–just briefly. The touch is so subtle that I feel stupid for the way it makes me feel–the way I can feel it everywhere.

She smiles softly, her lips pink and cheeks flushed.

"I think I'd like that, too."

Fourteen

Ellis

"You're just going to ride the tube." Ryan points to the tip of the tattoo gun. "See that plastic part there? Use that so you don't have to control the depth of the needle."

The machine turns on, and suddenly I'm regretting every decision I've ever made that led me up to this point. My heart is pounding in my chest as Ryan casually hands me a tattoo gun and tells me to have at it.

This can't be legal.

Every single direction Ryan gave me is running on repeat in my mind, so I don't forget a single one as I bring the needle down, slowly following the straight line until it all becomes too much. I pull the gun away.

"I can't do this," I say, shaking my head.

"Ellis," Griffin says, looking over my shoulder. "It's literally just an orange."

I stare down at the fruit on the table in front of me, the incomplete line splattered with ink because I haven't wiped away the excess. My hand is trembling, and Ryan lets out a laugh next to me, sitting back in his chair and running a hand down his face to hide his smile.

Griffin's warm eyes meet mine. "You're practicing on fruit. It's literally fine."

"I can't tattoo you," I say. "That's certifiably insane. I sketch in a sketchbook every so often. It's not the same."

"It's not," Ryan affirms. "But it's a start."

I look back at the orange, the buzzing of the tattoo gun still sounding from where I set it on the table.

"I'm pretty sure I'm not even allowed to be doing this," I say.

I feel the plastic bandage covering the back of my arm, pulling my sleeve up and taking a peek at my newest impulsive decision. The lines are thin—smooth. It looks exactly as it should. Beautiful flowers decorating a vintage bike—beauty blooming from the basket on the front. There's no way I can match that.

Griffin crouches down, bringing us eye-to-eye from where I sit. He looks concerned. "I'm not going to make you give me a tattoo," he says, his voice soft. One corner of his mouth turned up at the corner. "I only thought it would be fun since Ryan owns the shop, and you like drawing."

"What if I completely ruin your skin and make you the ugliest human alive?" I ask.

Finn's eyes brighten, dancing with humor. "Then good thing you already fake married me. I won't have to worry about being alone for the rest of my life."

I look back at the orange, biting my lip and contemplating what I actually want to do. If I were being honest, giving someone a tattoo definitely sounds like the type of activity you'd be crossing off your bucket list. It also seems pretty reckless.

I kind of want to be able to say I did it. Just for the hell of it.

"Okay, I'm going to do it," I announce with new determination.

Picking up the tattoo gun, I focus on my breathing, steadying my hand and readying myself to create some art. My mind is swimming with all the ways this could go wrong, but the excitement is searing through me–burning through my fear and making me feel like I could do anything.

I put the needle to the orange, and time slows. I find myself in my own little world, carefully crafting and creating and–

"There," I say.

Ryan snatches the fruit, examining my work. "You're not going to hurt him," he says.

I deadpan. "Encouraging."

Ryan tosses the orange to Griffin to let him analyze my work. He nods before throwing the fruit in the trash.

"It was a lovely straight line," Finn says. "I trust you completely."

Before we sat down to do this, just after Ryan finished my tattoo, I told him what I wanted to do. He quickly let me know that whatever

I etched into Finn's skin had to be the simplest design I could think up. It was pretty easy to decide, but Griffin still has no idea.

Before I know it, Finn is on his stomach, his shirt pulled off to reveal his back, free from the patchwork of tattoos that decorate his arms and legs.

"Just above my shoulder blade," he instructs. "And if you kill me, at least we had a good time."

Ryan starts prepping supplies, pausing to hand me a pen. "Just sketch it out real fast," he says. "You can follow the lines."

Griffin turns his head to the side, resting it on his arms to look at me. It's strange being this close to him—feeling this close to him when we've only known each other for less than twenty-four hours.

And now I'm about to mark his skin permanently.

"I'm going to try to guess what it is." A small dusting of stubble has formed on his face, and I wonder how often he has to shave. I wonder what his favorite color is—his favorite food. I want to know if he is a sock, sock, shoe, shoe person or a sock, shoe, sock, shoe person. If he's the latter, our friendship cannot continue past this tattoo shop.

"Okay," I say, uncapping the pen and running my fingers over his skin, trying to find the perfect spot.

He sucks in a sharp breath, and I watch as the muscles in his back tense and then relax.

"Sorry," I say, my voice low. "Are my hands cold?"

He's turned his head away, facing the other direction. Finn doesn't answer immediately, and I hear Ryan talking to someone one room over.

"No." His voice is nearly a whisper. "They're not cold."

My stomach flutters, and I don't ask any more questions.

I quickly sketch out the simple design, hoping that he won't be disappointed, but more importantly, hoping that I don't accidentally hurt him. I felt bad enough for the orange.

Once it's done, which doesn't take long, I set the pen down on the small tray next to me as Ryan makes his way to my side. I stare at the spot, wondering how he would be able to tell what I made in such a short amount of time. "Okay, give it a guess."

Finn turns to look at me again, and I notice the way his jaw ticks as if he's holding back a smile. "I'm not going to tell you, but I will say it's very obvious."

"That's not fair!" I swat at him. "You could lie and say you got it right. Tell me now."

"It's a crescent moon," he says, his tone assured.

I frown. "How did you know?"

The smile breaks free then. "Easy, Ellis. You'll have to try harder next time."

Next time.

"Alright," Ryan announces, and I hear the buzzing of the tattoo gun start up again, my palms instantly sweaty. "It's go time."

• • • • ● • ● • • •

The cold air swirls around us when we exit the tattoo shop. Christmas lights hang on the trees near the sidewalk and remind me of the season. I've hardly thought about the holiday—not with B gone.

I wonder if they have a special Christmas gathering for lonely people—the ones who have little to no friends outside of their job. A gathering for people with dead moms and unknown fathers who desperately need company for the holiday.

I briefly consider attending an AA meeting.

"Why are you frowning?" Finn asks, his hands tucked into the pocket of his sweatshirt. "I told you it looks great."

"It's not that." I don't want to admit what I'm thinking. It sounds pitiful. I don't want to sound like I'm asking for pity. He's already gone above and beyond to make my birthday special. In fact, I'm not sure anything else could top this weekend—not ever.

"What is it?" Finn nudges into me.

"I'm just surprised you let me participate in that level of body modification, is all." It's not the full truth, but it's enough. "Next thing you know, you'll be letting strange women dye your hair purple."

That same smile rests on his face—the one that makes his entire demeanor shift, and I briefly realize that I haven't been subjected to his RBF since the coffee shop.

"We could do that," he says. "It's just hair."

My brows lower. "You're not serious?"

We stand in front of his car in the parking lot of the tattoo parlor, eyes locked and ink freshly engraved into our skin.

"Oh, I'm very serious, Ellis." His tongue rolls along his cheek as he leans in ever so slightly, making my entire body feel at least ten degrees warmer. "I want to keep spending time with you."

"And you think letting me dye your hair is a good way to do that?"

He shrugs. "Maybe it's on my bucket list to dye my hair. You don't know."

He's standing close, smelling like that expensive cologne from the wedding. The scent of amber reminds me of his eyes, hazel and shining like he's having as much fun as I am. It's strange to think that someone dressed so casually, someone who spends a good amount of time sitting in the dim light of their closet mixing music, smells like that. It certainly isn't unpleasant though, and I find myself leaning in.

"Okay then, Finn. Let's go buy some hair dye."

• • • • ● • ● • ● • •

"Somehow, I'm more nervous about you standing over me with gloves in this bathroom than I was when we were in the tattoo shop."

I glance at the open container of purple hair dye and back to where Finn sits shirtless on his toilet. He looks good. A light dusting of hair decorates his toned chest, and I fight to keep my eyes from dipping lower. "Honestly, this is far safer. I've used hair dye plenty of times."

"So what do you do?" he asks. "Just like, put it on there?"

My mouth turns up at one corner, and I dig into the container with one gloved hand, pulling out a glob of purple. "Pretty much. Then we will wait for fifteen minutes and you'll rinse it out." I stare at his dark strands of hair, wondering if this is even worth it. "To be transparent, it may not be that different. This stuff is made for brown hair, but yours is pretty dark. It might not be that purple in the end."

Finn leans back a bit, eyes dancing with humor. "Perfect. I can't even pay you back because your hair is darker than mine."

"You have to think things through," I tease. "You've given me the upper hand."

He sits up, his legs relaxed and apart. Somehow, when I move to stand in between them, what we are doing starts to feel intimate. My stomach is fluttering again, my mind dizzy, and from this angle, I can see the plastic bandage poking out over his shoulder from the tattoo I gave him.

I stop thinking and start running my hands through his hair. Finn holds his eyes steady on mine, and I can't for the life of me meet that stare—not when my breathing is so shallow.

The longer I spend breathing the same air as Griffin, the more I think the oxygen is laced with hard drugs.

"Why are you letting me do this?" I ask, grabbing more dye and working it through the strands. "Running around and letting me give you tattoos, dye your hair, and force you to weddings you don't belong at."

Finn chuckles, casting his eyes downward. "It's fun," he offers, but I don't feel like that's the full extent of it. I dare a glance, and when he looks up, I can tell that it wasn't.

"My brother," he continues. "When he passed away, every holiday—birthday—every event. It all felt—" He pauses, trying to conjure up the right word. "Bigger somehow. Like any single one could be our last time together." His hands rest on his knees, and I briefly register the warmth radiating off his body. "When I saw your picture pop up and realized the coffee-covered girl from earlier didn't have anyone to spend her birthday with, I thought I'd jump in and take care of things."

I focus on his hair, nearly done considering the length. "That's–" My brow furrows. "That's sweet."

"Well, it was that and the fact that you're very pretty."

A laugh drags from my throat, and I lean back, keeping my feet firmly planted between his and refusing to talk about what he just confessed to. From the depths of my recent memory, I remember his comment about palming my ass and my cheeks suddenly heat.

I wish he would.

"Should be good to go," I say, carefully pulling the gloves from my hands, throwing them in the trash, and reaching toward the counter to set a timer on my phone. "Now we just have to wait. Maybe you can tell me more about this tight-knit family of yours. Considering most of what I know about you is a lie from the wedding."

Finn looks up, and I notice how long his eyelashes are. It's an insult to all women.

"I have one sister, Skylar. She lives in New York with her partner. She should actually be here on the twenty-fourth for Christmas. We will all be going to my parents' house."

I'm still standing between his legs, looking at the saturated strands of hair, and not really knowing what to do with myself or my hands. I risk touching him, my body buzzing as I tilt his head to the side, pretending to analyze my handiwork.

"And where do your parents live?" I ask.

"Thirty minutes away. It's a small town just east of here. They have some good restaurants that way. We could go check them out."

I pause, my hands still on his cheeks, his newfound stubble scratching beneath my skin as he stares at me. He's absolutely serious.

"If you needed another two-hundred dollars, Finn, you should have just said so."

He frowns, brows lowered, that smile disappearing, and I desperately want to bring it back. "It's not about the money. I just wanted to spend time with you. I spent all the other stuff between the thrift store, the wedding, and your tattoo anyway."

"How much was the tattoo?"

"A bit more than two-hundred dollars." His smirk returns, and warmth runs through my chest, pushing out to every limb as I stare at him.

The bathroom is silent aside from the gentle sound of the fan, keeping the dye fumes at bay while we stand and stare at each other like we've known one another forever.

When Finn's lips part, my stomach dips, and I risk moving closer—just a hair before his hands meet the backs of my thighs over the jeans I'm wearing.

Mouths parted, breaths heavy, his eyes dip down to my lips. I think for a moment that maybe hiring someone to plan my birthday wasn't that pitiful after all. He hasn't made me feel that way, at least.

"I want to kiss you, Ellis," he whispers. That warmth doubles and my entire body feels like it's on fire and suspended over a raging river—a river I would really like to drown in. "I just don't want you to compare me to a serial killer. You so clearly watch those crime documentaries and probably know how to fight back. I need to make sure this is okay."

His eyes are heated and vulnerable, chest rising and falling like the tide as I lean in. "It's okay," I answer, my voice so low I struggle to hear it.

It's all the confirmation he needs.

When his lips press against mine—gentle and seeking—I find myself lost to the feel of his hands dragging up higher on my thighs and pulling me in. My hands are on his chest, exploring the warmth of his skin and the muscles beneath.

That gentle pressure changes, becoming hungrier, and I almost bring my hands up to tangle them in his hair before I remember all the hair dye. I rest my hands around the back of his neck instead, pushing closer as a low rumble sounds from deep in his throat, spiking my blood with pure *want*.

I'm grappling for control, not sure I even want it when a horrible thought crosses my mind.

This is not a good idea.

This is reckless.

I pull away, staring down at his swollen lips, those insane eyelashes, and the way he looks like he just ran a marathon. "Sorry," I say, not really knowing what I'm apologizing for.

"For kissing me?" he asks, tilting his head to the side.

My brow furrows—an uncomfortable feeling stirring in my gut. It's like the old Ellis is creeping back in—the one that needs to be steady and responsible.

"For stopping," I clarify.

Finn lets out a breathy chuckle, placing his hands on his knees again and giving me the freedom to step away. I don't, though.

I don't want to be the old Ellis, either. I want to be whatever–whoever I am with him.

"You're welcome to stop," he says. "You're also welcome to walk out the door if you so choose, Ellis. Though I have to admit, I don't regret kissing you. Not in the slightest."

I smile, those feelings of doubt draining away at the softness in his deep voice, the way he's looking at me–confessing to feelings I'm having too. "Okay," I finally respond. "No more documentaries for me. You were right to guess that."

I lean down, throwing my entire being into the kiss. This time, that doubt is nowhere to be found as he brings his hands to the back of my legs and pulls me in. His touch is more demanding, as if I've given him permission to take more control, and I like it.

An involuntary noise sounds from my throat–dark and needy as his hands tighten on my thighs. My hands are all over his chest, his arms–mapping out the tattoos I've yet to ask questions about.

Griffin leans back. His fingers tighten, urging me forward. Without thinking, I move–straddling him while his tongue trails over my bottom lip.

He groans when my body lowers, his hands now firmly planted on my waist.

Breaking the kiss, he keeps his mouth just inches from mine. I want to drag him back to me.

"Shit," he mutters, and I'm suddenly aware that I'm on his lap feeling exactly what the kiss has done to him.

"Sorry," I whisper.

Finn shakes his head, his lip pulling up at the corner and creating one more smile for me to pocket and keep forever.

"Stop fucking apologizing, Ellie." His hands are in my hair–his tongue is in my mouth. I think the earth stopped spinning.

A deep ache catches me by surprise, and I find myself craving *friction*. Just before I give into the want completely, the timer goes off.

We both startle apart, and I glance at my phone. "Time's up," I say, my voice coming out more breathless than I intended. "We need to wash it out."

"Should I just wash it in the sink?" he asks.

I nod toward the shower before glancing at where my legs are wrapped around his waist. I pry myself off of him and take a step back. "I'll go out to the hall. It'll probably be easier if you wash it out in the shower."

Finn smiles, and it's the most devastating thing I've ever seen. This is the one I don't want to just pocket–I want to hang it on my wall and stare at it forever.

"There's a pizza in the freezer," he informs. "I think I trust you enough to put it in the oven. We can eat once my hair is purple."

I grab my phone, shoving it in my back pocket as I move toward the door. Finn stands up, and I'm reminded of his height again. It was easy to forget with him seated in front of me.

"Make pizza. Don't burn down the apartment complex. Got it."

"I'm trusting you, Ellie," he says, turning to start the water as I walk through the door and close it.

I can't wipe the smile off my face, pulling out my phone and finding Lennon's name.

Me: *Something happened*

Her response is almost immediate.

Lennon: *Spill, bitch. Don't make me fly back home. You know I'm too poor for that.*

I walk into the kitchen, find the frozen pizza, and start the oven before typing out my response.

Me: *I kissed him. And I think I like him more than I like those homemade pop-tarts that taste like apple pie at the coffee shop we went to on Thursday.*

Simon jumps up onto the counter, and I fight to protect the pizza by quickly unwrapping it, finding a pan, and shoving it into the oven before the thing even preheats. I add an extra two minutes to the cook time and hope it makes up for it.

Lennon: *Shit. I don't have the money to be a bridesmaid.*
Me: *Oh my god, would you just chill?*
Lennon: *Never*

Fifteen

Griffin

Looking in the mirror, I wipe my hand across the surface to reveal exactly what I should have expected.

Purple hair.

I lean closer, trying to get a clear picture of what I've just done—or had Ellis do, rather. As it turns out, it's not overwhelmingly purple. She was right that it wouldn't be out there—just a subtle deep purple color that every single one of my friends is going to be sure to notice and give me shit for.

I rub the towel over my hair as my phone buzzes from where it sits on the counter. Answering the call, I put my phone on speaker and lean forward, running my fingers through the newly dyed strands in an attempt to appear somewhat presentable for the girl I just made out with in my bathroom.

"Where have you been?" Noah's voice echoes off the walls. "You've answered next to no text messages since yesterday. I'm very close to filing a missing persons report."

"I'm with Ellis." I throw the towel over the hanger, then pull it back off to fold it and hang it appropriately. I pick my briefs up off the floor and pull them on before my jeans.

"You're shitting me."

Grabbing my T-shirt off the floor too, I look at my hair again. He's definitely going to give me shit when he hears about this—or sees it—whichever comes first.

"I'm not," I say. "I like her. She's cool." It's the understatement of the century.

I kissed a lot of girls after I turned sixteen. It was before Storm died. But after I lost my brother, relationships took on more meaning—not just the family ones. I've dated three girls seriously since then, and I can't remember a single kiss. Not after I sat in my bathroom with Ellis's fingers trailing over my skin—her lips on mine. I can still feel her step closer when my palms met the back of her thighs—still feel the overwhelming desire to move my hands higher, and the paralyzing fear that doing anything more might cause me to fuck it all up. It was like standing on a bridge and waiting to jump.

And then she fucking straddled me.

"Well, I'm thinking we could go for dinner tonight at that bar off of High Street. Figured I'd invite Ryan." I can hear something shuffle in the background, then the closing of a car door, the jingle of keys.

I briefly consider inviting Ellis, but hold back. I'm not even sure she wants to hang out with me anymore. Maybe I'm being too intense. "That should be fine." I wince. This girl gave me money to plan her birthday, and I'm out here kissing her in my bathroom and letting her give me tattoos. She's probably run off by now. "Hey, I need to go."

"You guys aren't–"

"No, Noah. Keep your eggplant emojis to yourself, okay?"

Noah's laugh sounds like he sure as hell doesn't believe me.

I hang up the phone and walk out of the bathroom door, moving down the hallway until I find Ellis in the living room curled up on the couch with her phone in her hand. "The pizza should be done in exactly thirty seconds." A wide smile splits her face when she sees me, eyes lingering on my hair briefly. "You have impeccable timing." She pauses, pocketing her phone before stretching out her legs and moving to stand. "And you have purple hair."

Simon hops down from where he had been seated next to her, prowling across the room until he props himself in front of the sliding back door. I don't miss the way he glared at her—like he wasn't ready to give up his spot cuddled in close.

"I see my cat is whoring himself out to you. I don't know when he became so fond of strangers."

She stops in front of me, eyes shining when she looks up. "Don't judge your cat. You kissed me while sitting on a literal toilet with purple dye in your hair."

I laugh, the deep sound booming through my apartment. "I'd do it again."

The timer goes off for the pizza, and I spin on my heel, looking back once as Ellis follows me into the kitchen. I turn off the oven, grab a mitt, and pull out a frozen pizza.

"You didn't catch my house on fire," I state, grabbing the pizza cutter and working to divide our lunch

Ellis lets out an amused huff. "Of course, I didn't burn the house down." She grabs two plates from the cabinet and sets them on the counter. "How can you insult me like this? You let me dye your hair and draw a permanent crescent moon on your back, but you don't trust me to make a pizza?" Her tone is laced with humor, and when I look at her, she's smiling still, a dimple peeking out on her left cheek.

And damn if it doesn't make me go soft.

Ryan and Noah are going to absolutely slaughter me.

I throw a few pieces of pizza on each plate and turn to face her. "I never did ask about the tattoo. Why a crescent moon?"

Her cheeks flush, and she looks away. I decide that particular shade of pink might be my new favorite color. "It was a simple design," she says. "That and because we spent all night together. I don't know. It seemed fitting. Don't attach too much meaning to it." She finally looks at me, and my heart leaps in my chest as I try to put zero meaning to it. Absolutely none. No meaning. "You can pretend it has no meaning if you want. It's *your* poorly done tattoo."

I can't help the crooked smile on my face. I'm sure it's a dopey expression. "It's officially my second favorite tattoo."

She cocks an eyebrow. "Your *second* favorite?"

I lean against the counter, gazing down at her insulted expression, that humor still swirling in her brown eyes. "My brother will come back from the dead and haunt me with his freaky anime porn if I make your tattoo my favorite." We're standing close in my kitchen, and I can feel her fingers brush against mine, drawing me in closer. "I find that his ability to haunt me is more dangerous than your affinity for the color purple."

Ellis's eyes are bright. "It looks good, by the way." She reaches up, running her fingers through the still damp strands, analyzing her work. I want to pull her close again–to feel her skin on mine.

Fuck.

I cannot be hard right now.

"You think?" I grab her plate from behind me, holding it between us to offer it to her. "I think maybe you're right, Ellie. You should quit cricket farming and take up a job as a hairstylist."

When she grabs the plate, moves it to the side, and quickly presses a kiss to the corner of my mouth, my eyes widen. With her plate still in her hand, she spins to walk into the living room.

"I'm actually pretty hungry," she tosses over her shoulder.

I grab my pizza, following after her to the couch. I'd follow her to a lot of places. Maybe even all of them.

I throw myself on the couch next to her. "Then what in the world were you doing kissing me, my darling wife of over ten years?"

Ellis rolls her tongue along her cheek, curling her legs up with her plate balanced on her knees. She shrugs. "I like the purple."

. . . . ● . ● . . .

Ellis spent a lot of time talking about her aunt's daughter and telling me about how much her job sucks the life out of her. I made sure to mention that I wasn't surprised, and she glared at me and reminded me that arrogance looks good on no one–even if their hair is purple and they have an incredibly impressive crescent moon tattoo on their back.

As the afternoon stretches on toward dinner, I can't help but think I don't want our time to end. I'd be willing to take her on a thousand more adventures if only to get the chance to learn more about her life–her world.

It feels like I've gotten all the borders of the puzzle placed, and now I'm just getting to the good part–high on everything I've accomplished so far.

Ellis sits up, tucking a strand of hair behind her ear. "I should probably get going," she says, and I hate the way my heart sinks. "I probably smell disgusting, and these jeans were on wear number two when I put them on. I need to go home and change."

"You don't smell disgusting." I don't miss the way her eyes flick to my lips from where she now stands. "I'm supposed to meet Ryan and Noah for dinner, anyway." I reach over to pet Simon before standing up to walk her out.

Ellis grabs her bag by the door. "How would you know?" she challenges. "Your nostrils are filled with the scent of hair dye. You're probably still high off the fumes. That's why you started kissing strangers and stuff."

"You're not a stranger, Ellie." I'm standing next to her by the door, not quite ready for her to leave and leaning against the door frame. "Not anymore, at least." I lean against the wall, folding my arms across my chest. "And I promise you I was stone-cold sober when I kissed that beautiful mouth of yours."

Ellis stares at me, her bag in her hands, and her expression unreadable until I catch the soft smirk pull at her lips.

"Go on another adventure with me?"

Her eyes widen, and she seems surprised, but quickly recovers. "Okay," the bag sways in her hand, her eyes looking toward the ground as her cheeks grow pink. Is she embarrassed that I called her mouth beautiful? Was that too much?

"When?" she asks.

"Tuesday. Your actual birthday. Take the day off, and we can hang out."

Her eyes flick to mine, narrowing in suspicion. "I can't just take the day off."

"Yes, you can. People call off work on their birthday all the time."

"What would we even do?"

I think back to her bucket list, now memorized and firmly tattooed inside my brain—just like the crescent moon at my back. "How about Broadway?"

Ellis chuckles. "We can't go to New York, Finn."

"No," I confirm, "But I'll figure something out. Who knows, mabe New York will work out. You own a multi-million dollar cricket bar company. You probably have a private jet."

"I do not." She says the words with a laugh.

I chew on my cheek, promising her the same thing I'm promising myself. "We could go to Wyoming. I'd like to watch you ride a bull." I catch my mistake before she can even react. "Wholesomely. In a way I wouldn't be ashamed to tell my mother about."

She laughs then, and I want to bottle the sound. "Okay," she whispers. Her eyes linger on my lips, and I think for a moment she might kiss me again, but something in the air shifts, and she steps back. "Thank you, Griffin."

I clear my throat, shoving my hands in my pocket nervously and stepping away from the door. Maybe I fucked it up. I'm afraid I've fucked it up. Noah would tell me I've fucked it up. "Not Finn?" I ask.

Ellis's soft smile has me relaxing a bit when she answers. "I think I'd like to go bull riding." My worries ease. "And nobody calls you that."

There's a pause—a moment of silence stretching between us as I let her words sink in and hold her gaze, hoping she knows I like the new nickname. I like it a lot.

"You do," I say, and I swear her breath catches in her throat. "I'll see you on Tuesday?"

Ellis opens the door. "Absolutely."

Sixteen

Ellis

Staring at the ceiling of the small cape cod house I bought with all my stable job money, I contemplate running to the store to buy more popsicles.

Those seem to be my go to pity party food.

Sometime in the middle of reminiscing over the last two days, I forgot to skip ahead to the part where Finn parted my lips with his own, and got stuck somewhere in the middle of the scene in his apartment where he reminded me of the truth that I've refused to admit.

I hate my damn job.

When I graduated from college with my marketing degree, I did my best to find a position quickly. The hope was that I would fall into something stable, and I did. It's the same job I have now, and it's exactly that–stable.

You aren't passionate about marketing.

He was right–I'm not.

I sigh, dragging myself off the tan couch cushions and grabbing my phone from the end table. My stomach growls, and I grab a yogurt cup just before popping a piece of fancy sourdough bread I found at the grocery store into the toaster.

My phone sounds while I'm stuffing strawberry flavored sugar and dairy into my face, but I don't really care because it's Lennon.

Her face fills the small screen on my phone, faint sounds of dishes clinking in the background behind where she sits on the couch. I see her mom open the fridge somewhere behind her, and for what it's worth, she doesn't look like she's projectile vomiting.

"What would happen if I quit my job?" I start, skipping a greeting.

Lennon's smile stretches slowly across her freckled face and she pops what looks like a gummy bear into her mouth. "Hello." she says. "How are you, Ellis? How has life been? Did you get railed?"

"Shush!" I whisper yell. Balancing my phone against the vase of flowers on my kitchen counter, I shake my head. "I can see your mom in the background!"

"Oh, please!" Lennon cackles, tilting her head back. "Stella doesn't mind. Do you mom?"

Her mom pops into the frame, leaning over the back of the couch. Lennon is the spitting image of her mother. Stella smiles and wrinkles form at the corners of her eyes. Her hair is pulled back into a claw clip, and her skin doesn't look sallow in the slightest. The picture of health. "Is that Ellis Smalley? My favorite of my daughter's best friends."

"She's lying!" Lennon shoves her face closer to the phone, blocking her mom out. "You're my only best friend. I'm not whoring myself out, I swear. You, on the other hand—"

Stella snorts, and I feel like I might be having a hot flash. "Lennon," I warn, but she only responds by cackling.

"Okay, so you want to quit your job all of a sudden. What has the boy done to you? Was it that huge?"

I roll my eyes, but I know my cheeks are flaming. Stella takes that as her cue to go back to the other side of the room. "We just kissed. And I am just realizing I literally hate marketing. It's the worst, and while I love Rupert and Mallory is a decent boss, I hate the smell of tuna, the dungeon, and—"

"What does tuna have to do with it?" she asks. I wave a hand.

"Not important. I just think I want to do something else."

"So, do it." Lennon's smile has softened into a pleasant expression. There's nothing behind her green eyes but belief and hope—not a single worry to be found.

"I can't."

She pulls her phone down, and I can hear tapping on the screen. I'm left with the unsightly image of the inside of Lennon's nostrils. "Sure you can," she adds. "It's literally your life. You can quit your job and move to Peru. You can keep your job and find a second outlet, something you're passionate about. The world is wide open. Also, don't think we won't be discussing this kiss. Did he use tongue?"

I ignore her question, furrowing my brows. She's always like this—thinking things are simple and easy. If Lennon wants to do something, she just does it. Her job at the pediatric office nearby is temporary. Lennon has her sights set on buying an old house and converting it into a bed and breakfast. I have no doubt she will do it, too.

"Why am I looking up your nostrils right now?" The toaster pops, and I realize I've just created coal. I might as well be Santa's supplier for all the kids that wipe boogers on their school papers.

"I'm going to order you some ice cream and have it delivered." Lennon is still typing on her phone as I try to fish out two pieces of toast that I'm certain are the same temperature as the sun.

"I'll just order my own ice cream," I say.

Lennon snorts. "You better fucking not. It's almost your birthday, let me buy you ice cream, you heinous bitch."

"I'm already there." I'm not. I don't have the app pulled up at all, but I know it'll irritate her.

"Don't do it. I swear to God."

A smile tugs at the corner of my mouth. "I'd swear to Jesus instead. He seemed more chill. The God of the Old Testament might give you leprosy."

"Jesus would give you leprosy, too."

I briefly consider buying myself a second pint of ice cream anyway. One can be for my mid-life crisis about my hopes and dreams, and the other can be for celebrating Finn's firm backside. It's the eighth wonder of the world.

"Jesus would cure my leprosy, Lennon."

"*I'm* threatening to give *you* leprosy!" Lennon's tiny face in the corner of my phone lights up. "Besides, you'll have ice cream in twenty-minutes. Don't order it for yourself. Also, we did our family Christmas thing and I'll be home on Wednesday."

"Then I can tell you about making out with audio boy on a toilet."

Lennon visibly recoils. Her face twists into something shocked, appalled, and disgusted. The very image of *I hate everything about what you just said.*

It pulls a laugh deep from the pit of my belly. "It's not what you're thinking."

"Listen," Lennon begins. "I've read several kinky romance books, and this is still very new. Did you–" Lennon pretends to gag. "Did you like that?"

"The kiss?" I say. "Yes, very much so. I was dying his hair purple. He wasn't taking a shit or anything."

Lennon squeaks. "Purple hair? Am I attracted to this?"

I can't fight the dopey smile on my face. It gives away everything, and I realize that I still haven't texted Mallory to call off on Tuesday. "He's so hot, Lennon. But I *do* have to go."

"Okay, okay. I will accost you with questions on Wednesday when we hang out, and I promise to bribe you with wine. Enjoy your ice cream."

"I will."

When I hang up, I pull up Mallory's contact and shoot her a text about Tuesday. I never call off, so it really shouldn't be a problem.

Finding that I have an overwhelming urge to text Griffin, I remember that we never exchanged numbers. Instead, I thumb my way to the freelance site where I hired him and see that I have a message already there—sent exactly six seconds ago.

Impeccable timing.

GJPAudio: *I forgot to give you my number. Any girl who kisses like that should have it.*

I pull the phone to my chest like I'm some ridiculous *not like other girls* character in a cheesy romantic comedy. The reality is that I'm very much like other girls. I listen to Taylor Swift, love Target, and went through that weird social media phase where everyone was taking pictures of their food and applying terrible filters.

When I go to look at the message again, it's gone but quickly replaced by a new one.

GJPAudio: *The app flagged my message because I said "kisses." Here's my number again.*

GJPAudio: *Fuck, I said kisses again. It's going to disappear.*

I quickly click on the number and add it to my contacts before typing out a text message. For some reason, nerves rise in the pit of my belly. I am thankful I didn't try to eat my charcoal toast. I would have probably thrown it up all over my clean counters.

Me: *Don't worry. I got your number.*

It doesn't take long for him to respond to my text, and I find myself giddy—smiling like an absolute idiot and dreading the fact that I have to return to work tomorrow.

Finn: *Good, because I can't send any more messages on the app for twenty-four-hours.*
Me: *What will that do to all your fantastic ratings?*
Finn: *They'll probably disappear, and I'll be forced to quit music.*
Me: *But you look so pretty playing piano. I'm going to leave you five stars right now.*

There's a brief pause before he responds again, and I'm left feeling the ghost of his kiss on my mouth. I would do it again.

Finn: *You think I'm pretty?*
Me: *Not sure. I'll reevaluate on Tuesday.*
Finn: *Can't wait.*

Seventeen

Griffin

"What the hell are you smiling at?"

Noah's voice draws my attention away from my phone, and I look up, returning to the present.

We decided to head to the local bar where we ordered food and planned on moving to the plethora of arcade games. The bar is one of my favorites because games are included with the purchase of any beer or mixed drink.

Noah has a brow raised with his mouth pulled into a knowing smirk.

"What do you mean?" I ask, sliding my phone back into my pocket and pulling the beer to my lips.

Lips that Ellis kissed hours ago.

Fuck.

"You're staring at your phone wearing a grin that screams *I'm simping for a girl I just met.* I know that look." Noah taps a finger on the rustic wooden table before grabbing his own beer. "I thought you said no sex."

Ryan sits next to him, scrolling through his phone with an expression that tells me he is definitely listening to the conversation. He grabs a garlic knot from the center of the table and pops it in his mouth.

"We didn't have sex," I say because it's the truth, though I'm positive they don't believe me.

"*Finn* let the girl give him a tattoo." Ryan finally looks up from his phone, adjusts the beanie on his head, and leans back in his chair. "Like in my shop with my tattoo gun."

"Is that even legal?" Noah asks.

I can still feel the bandage on my shoulder, the reminder of my time with Ellis. It's a memory I'm happy to have engraved into my skin. In fact, I want to go on making more memories with the girl. I need to see her again.

Fighting the temptation to pull my phone out and send her another text, I distract myself by grabbing a garlic knot for myself. If I'm eating, maybe they won't expect an answer.

"It's only illegal if we talk about it," Ryan says, while grabbing his beer and taking a swig. "And look at him," he continues. "Suddenly the guy has purple hair. How did that happen, Griffin?"

"Yeah, Griffin. Why is your hair dark purple?"

The shit-eating grins they both wear remind me of Skylar's face when we were younger. The expression she wore when she knew I was about to take the fall for whatever she'd done.

"Ellis dyed it," I answer honestly, around a mouthful of food.

The sounds of the bar become louder as I wait for their response. I can hear glasses clinking from behind the counter, murmurs of people talking, and the music blasting over the speakers and mixing with the sounds of arcade games.

Noah turns to Ryan, and I swear for grown ass men, they have certainly become the worst gossips in the world. They're not even good at it–considering I'm sitting right in front of them.

"He just met this chick yesterday," Noah tells him. "Hired him to plan her birthday, and now he's acting like she hung the moon and stars specifically for him."

"No shit," Ryan says, his eyes bright. "I mean, he's never done anything halfway. Especially not his women."

"Fuck you guys, I'm literally right here." I toss a garlic knot across the table at Noah, and he raises his hands in defense.

"No need to get aggressive, *Finn*. If you kill me, my mother's grudge will be so large she'll stop making pho for your family."

Ryan whistles, his face scrunching. "Ouch, Finn. Better get it together."

I knew that they'd both give me shit for Ellis. Ryan and Noah know my history–my past–and they know about my former relationships. Unlike Noah, I don't usually date. When my brother died, it didn't feel worth it to fuck around anymore. And even though they're right to mention that I just met this girl, it doesn't mean I'm not interested.

I am sure as shit interested.

I give up and pull my phone out, rolling my eyes before taking another drag from my beer bottle.

Me: *I found something online earlier. Dress country.*

Her response is almost instant, and I can't pretend it doesn't light up my chest.

Ellis: *Country? What is that supposed to mean?*
Me: *Jeans, cowboy boots. Something like that, I guess.*
Ellis: *Got it, boss. Cowgirl country.*

When I look up, my friends are still staring at me. It's starting to feel like I'm wearing all of my emotions on a big sign hanging around my neck.

"What?" I ask.

Noah speaks first. "Okay, lover boy. You ready to have your ass handed to you in Pacman?"

"He might be so distracted by his new girl that winning will be a piece of cake," Ryan adds.

I pocket my phone and suck down the last of my drink before glancing at the games surrounding us. Both Ryan and Noah know I'm a Pacman champion, and the only asses about to be handed are their own.

When their chairs scratch across the hard floors, the thrill of competition runs through my veins, reminding me of why I agreed to go out with the two of them at all–even if I knew the shit they'd give me.

I point at both of them. "You fuckers are going down."

· · · ●·●·● · ·

After a late night with Noah and Ryan, I spent the rest of the evening pissed that I couldn't get any jobs freelancing because of my messaging ban, but also not as pissed as I could have been because I'd gotten Ellie's number.

I worked through the night on her song, trying to make it perfect. Truth be told, she had a fucking fantastic voice. Her drawings were also well done, her hair soft. I thought about the way it felt through my fingers at least four times before I realized I'd tented my damn basketball shorts and started feeling pathetic.

I gave up and went to bed.

Walking up the concrete walkway to my parents' house, I can't shake the excitement of the date I have planned for tomorrow. I talked to my mom on the phone earlier, so she knew I'd be coming home. It was, however, a mistake because I also had to swing by Noah's and pick up more food.

When I open the door, Tom Petty blasts through the speakers toward the back of the house where my mom's sunroom is located. She had better windows and a heater installed so she could use it all year round.

I kick my shoes off, careful not to tip the containers in the bag I carry as I make my way to where my mother is singing and dancing with a paintbrush in her hand.

Wild strands of curly dark hair escape from the bun stacked on top of her head. She wipes a paintbrush on her linen overalls, oblivious to my presence.

"Hey, Mom." I say it by way of greeting.

She spins, paintbrush pointed at me like a weapon. Her scowling highlights the wrinkles on her forehead as she glances down to the bag of food in my hand. "If that's not the food I asked for, you can turn around and leave now, son."

I smile, walking forward to draw her in for a hug. She accepts and wraps one arm around my back. There's just something about it–home and family. It's like every time I step into this house I'm filled with memories of laughter and music–dancing in the kitchen with my father while my mother watches him cook.

There are bad memories, too. They're the cloudy gray ones that came when Storm died, but I try not to think about those too much. It doesn't do me any good to remember my mother's tears–or my dad's.

"It's exactly what you asked for, Mom. I wouldn't steer you wrong."

She grabs the food, tossing her paintbrush into an old coffee can filled with water and decorated with dried paints before passing me to go to the kitchen.

I follow.

"So," she begins, opening the fridge to put the food away. "You said something about wanting to borrow your dad's old cowboy hat?"

I lean over the kitchen island, elbows firmly planted as I take in the familiarity of home. Incense and cinnamon–a poor attempt at covering up the smell of paint in the air. Tom Petty has turned into Norah Jones, and I can do nothing but take it all in–soak it up.

"Yeah, I'm taking a girl to a bar tomorrow."

My mom's brows furrow. "A bar? Honestly, Griffin." She does a terrible job of hiding how judgmental she is of what I just announced. Apparently, a bar is a terrible idea for a date in June Peterson's eyes.

It's not a date, though. And I need to keep reminding myself of that.

"They have a mechanical bull. It's something on her bucket list, I just wanted to dress the part."

The statement seems to appease her, and she nods, digging into one of the drawers for a spoon. My mom turns back to the fridge and grabs the bag of food.

"I'm just going to have this now," she says. "Also, if it's on her bucket list, then the bar is very thoughtful, Griffin." She pops the lid off the container and throws it into the microwave. "It should be somewhere in that bin in the basement. No telling what you'll find down there. Do you want to stay and split this with me?"

"Sure, Mom." I smile, rounding the island to look at the bag of food I delivered. I'm not sure what anything is, but every time I've gone to Noah's parents' house, I've enjoyed everything I ate. "Don't let me forget the cowboy hat," I add. "It's important."

She smiles, a knowing expression etched into her features. "Of course."

We stand around the island eating when I notice the air shift, my mom's brows furrowing.

"Skylar called," she starts, and a knot forms in my stomach.

"Is something wrong?" I ask on instinct.

She shakes her head, a soft chuckle escaping her lips. "No, no. Nothing like that. She's really enjoying New York." There's a pause, one weighted like lead, and I can't help but wonder where the conversation is going.

"You used to want to leave once," she starts. I can't help but poke at my food, the icy wall around the idea forming in my heart. That dream is long gone. I couldn't bear to move from family–from home.

"I was a kid."

"Well," she says, "most dreams start when you're a kid. It's not often they just disappear." My mom reaches out a hand, covering mine on the counter. "I'm not trying to pester you. I just love you, Griffin. If you want to pursue seeing the world, I think you should. You don't have to stay here. While I talked to your sister, I realized how happy she sounded." Her hand warms mine as something tugs in my chest.

Maybe she isn't wrong. It *was* a dream. Some of the ice thaws, but I still keep the idea locked away. There haven't been any touring opportunities falling in my lap. I like my stable job. I like my life.

"You know," she adds after a moment of silence, "I just want to see you happy."

I smirk, trying to reassure her. The past few days I have been happy, so it's not like I'm lying. I've been inexplicably happy. "I appreciate that."

She grabs her bowl and sets it in the sink, returning to her spot at the island after rinsing it. "Let's go grab that cowboy hat."

My smile is genuine as I cock an eyebrow in her direction.

"Yee-haw."

Eighteen

Ellis

Finn showed up at my house around ten in the morning with a cup of coffee and a breakfast sandwich ready and waiting inside his Jeep.

We drove to his apartment where we sat close together watching the Broadway version of *The Lion King* on his television. Unfortunately, my cricket business didn't make enough for me to afford a private plane to New York. Even so, I think the show I got was far superior, anyway.

He took me out for lunch, where I learned more about his family, his favorite television shows, and the music he enjoys listening to.

Despite all his answers, he still refused to tell me why I was wearing cowboy boots and why he had a cowboy hat resting in the back seat of his car.

The endless road stretches out in front of us as Finn steers his car through backroads. He turns down the radio and reaches behind the passenger seat to pull out a small purple gift bag filled with tissue paper.

When I catch the crooked smirk on his face, my heart nearly stops.

"I got you something," he says as he places the bag on my lap, his eyes flicking between the road and my face. "It's a birthday gift."

I chuckle, running my fingers over the delicate tissue paper and listening to his frustrated grunt.

"Well, open it, Ellie."

I laugh, tossing tissue paper into his otherwise pristine car. I dig into the bag, my fingers brushing against a book, and I immediately know what it is before I pull it out.

"A new sketchbook?" I say, turning toward him, and I can tell he's pleased with himself.

Finn's fingers tighten on the steering wheel, and for a moment I see the doubt flicker in his eyes. It's silly because my chest feels so warm it could burst, and I can't believe I ever thought about buying more popsicles. At this rate, I can't imagine experiencing pitiful sorrow ever again.

"It's not much," he says. I swear I see a light pink color decorate his cheeks. "But I wanted you to open something on your birthday."

I reach over, gently prying one hand off the steering wheel and threading my fingers through his. Finn offers me another one of his show stopping smiles and presses his lips to the back of my hand as the road turns to gravel. My stomach somersaults when I notice just how far out from the city we are.

"Where are we going?"

Finn places his elbow on the console and lowers his hand, but his fingers never let go. "I hope you like dancing."

It's the only answer he gives me before we pull down a long dirt road. The bare trees climb up toward the gray sky, their leaves rustling and dry on the ground where they wait to be absorbed into the earth.

I look through the trees and watch the gentle sway of the branches when we pass them.

At the end of the road, a large steel building rests nestled between the trees, with a large sign hanging from a wooden post stuck in the ground. The sign is void of any lettering, which would make me nervous. I'm in too deep now—got too comfortable around Finn. If he did have Ted Bundy vibes, this would have been the perfect ruse. Spend two days getting me to trust him just to murder me out in the middle of the woods.

All of that *would* worry me if I hadn't noticed the giant handlebar mustache painted on the sign. It wouldn't make a very good place to kill a woman. It would be too comical.

"The Handlebar Ranch," he says, and I realize it makes perfect sense.

With the mustache and all.

Finn puts the car in park and turns toward me. "It wasn't necessarily on your bucket list, but I signed us up for swing dancing lessons. I was also told that after six, they start up the mechanical bull they rented. They being whoever is hosting this event. I don't know these people, but I figured–" He cuts himself off as he reaches behind my seat to the back of his car, grabbing his cowboy hat and placing it firmly on his head. I watch the flex of his biceps where his T-shirt ends, and draw my eyes back up to his face. "I figured it would be a lot nicer to look like this in front of people we don't know. I have a couple of flannels in the back, too. So, we can really dress the part."

I'm staring at him, my heart beating steadily in my chest as I watch this purple-haired cowboy with tattoos and an aversion to country music look at me with nothing but hope in his eyes.

And if I'm honest, he's gone above and beyond.

"You said you have multiple flannels?" I ask, and Finn nods. "Then I better ditch the sweater and get into character."

Finn chuckles, grabbing the shirts from the floor of the backseat and handing me a dark blue and white plaid flannel. He unbuckles his seatbelt and shrugs his own green and brown flannel over his shoulders, making quick work of the buttons and bouncing his knee nervously.

There are plenty of cars in the small parking lot around the ranch, and my stomach flutters with nerves. At least we won't know anyone in the bar. I've never tried to swing dance before, so I'm assuming I'll be terrible. It's only fair.

Making sure to pull my tank top down, I drag my dark green sweater over my head and replace it with the shirt Finn gave me. It's a bit big, so I give up on the buttons and tie the thing just above the high-waisted jeans I'm wearing, cowboy boots from the thrift store firmly attached to my feet.

When I look up at Griffin, he's staring at me, his eyes glancing down toward the lower cut of my tank top before meeting my eyes again.

It's like his gaze shoots fire on my skin wherever it lands, and I find that it's suddenly more difficult to breathe. The car is entirely too small. There's not enough oxygen, and for some reason, it feels like August instead of December.

I'm thinking about the kiss again.

"Well," I say, trying to break the tension. "We'd better get inside."

Finn shakes his head, his grin returning before he rushes out of the car and sprints to my side to open my door. As soon as my boots hit the dirt, I grab his hand in mine and we walk into The Handlebar Ranch together.

· • • • • • • • • • ·

Griffin Peterson is terrible at swing dancing.

Wes, the instructor they brought in keeps coming by to check on us. I swear the man laughs every time he listens to my dance partner firmly insisting that we are going to do some insane dip that I definitely don't feel safe trying.

Not when Finn can't even move his feet in the right direction.

Wes lingers a few feet away, his brown eyes observant, an amused smile threatening to break across his face and reveal all the hilarious judgment he's passing on both of us.

"Listen, Finn. When we are facing one another, the left is going to be on the same side." Even with his terrible dancing, I can't help but laugh at his hilarious jokes, his determination, and the way he doesn't seem to care what the entire class seems to think of him.

Not that it's difficult to ignore the opinions of people who decorated the venue with various pieces of taxidermy dressed like Santa.

"I'm hearing what you're saying," he says, as he takes a step back, clasping my hands firmly before bringing our arms up and out as we move forward together. "But I'm just not fully understanding. Now spin, Ellie. We gotta make this look good."

I laugh as one of his arms rises above my head, his hand gently guiding me to turn until I'm standing with my back firmly against his chest. His arms are still holding me there, and while the music around us continues, Griffin does not.

"What's going on there, Cowboy?" I tease, allowing myself to lean into him.

I can feel his breath on the back of my neck when he huffs out a laugh. "I don't remember what direction you go after this."

I giggle, my eyes meeting the instructor's as he shakes his head and walks off. Finding another couple to help, I suppose.

"I think he's given up on us," I whisper. "We are too terrible at this."

When Finn leans down, my body still tightly tucked into his, my pulse quickens. I'm reminded of the kiss all over again and how much I want to repeat the entire thing. I'd even be willing to find another toilet if we must. Lennon's judgment be damned.

"He's given up on us, Ellie," he affirms. "We are a lost cause." His hands let go of mine, moving to grip my shoulders over the flannel he gave me, but he doesn't move.

"I rather like this shirt," I say, trying to hide the way my voice sounds breathless–the winding tension in my lower stomach. I can't be this close to him right now.

"Thanks," he says, and I can feel his smirk. "It's my dad's."

Whipping around to face him, I note the look on his face and realize he wasn't lying. "You gave me your dad's shirt for this? That's not romantic at all!"

Griffin's grin widens. "I didn't realize this was supposed to be romantic." He steps forward, looking down into my eyes. I can see the green flecks in his, the hazel color shining brightly. Fairy lights look good on Griffin Peterson, that's for damn sure.

"Well, I mean–" I don't finish the sentence, a flush of embarrassment slowly working to my cheeks as I realize what I just said. We kissed the other day, but it hasn't happened again. I'm not entirely sure I know what's happening between us. All I know is that I can't get enough of it.

"If you wanted romance, why didn't you just tell me?" Finn lifts his hand to gently run those long fingers along my cheek and my breath catches in my throat. He's leaning closer, lips inches from mine.

I can smell his spearmint gum, and I'm pretty sure I'd give anything to get closer.

Finn doesn't move, his mouth hovering just near mine as he whispers. "I'll give you romance, Ellie," he whispers. "I can't imagine giving it to anyone else right now."

I wait for the kiss to come, but it doesn't. I'm left hopelessly frustrated as Finn takes a step back, smiling in a way that makes me want to drag him closer and wipe the expression right off his face.

Wes marches his boots up the stairs and onto the stage at the far end of the ranch, his cowboy hat looking slightly more fitting than the one on Finn's head. I use that as my chance to grab it, placing it on my head instead.

"Looks better on you," Finn says, wrapping his arm around my back and pulling me to stand closer to him.

"Well, folks," Wes announces, with a microphone now firmly clasped in one hand. His deep drawl echoes through the entire space. "That concludes our swing dancing lessons today. We sure hope you stick around for the rest of our Country Christmas celebration. Drinks are available at the bar, and Josh is headed over to the back of the room to start up that there mechanical bull. If your legs aren't tired, you might want to take it for a spin."

With that last statement, he's staring at us, and I'm now certain we are the worst swing dancers in the entire county. We are the ones with the tired legs.

"The mechanical bull," I say, turning to my head to face Finn. I'm certain the excitement in my eyes is shining so brightly, he'll be blinded in no time. "'Bout time I got to ride something."

Finn does something that falls somewhere between choking on his own spit, and laughing. I'm not sure which it is, but whatever he's done, it immediately makes me think back on my words and regret them with a vengeance.

I turn away, my body flaming like the sun. It's the type of embarrassment that burns so hot it outshines any other emotion you may have been having before–if only for a moment.

When Griffin sees my reaction, his grip tightens on my waist just briefly.

"'Bout time," he repeats.

Nineteen

Griffin

I bought Ellis a hard seltzer from an old woman tending the bar directly below the giant bear's head hanging on the wall with Christmas lights wrapped around him. I'm not sure if the decor was meant to be festive, or threatening. The bear looked like he was being held hostage by a giant glowing rope.

Ellis named him Herold.

Standing in line for the worn down mechanical bull, I find two very important truths. One, driving an hour out to a country Christmas celebration in the middle of nowhere is a fantastic idea. The second thing I realize is Ellis looks damn good in a cowboy hat.

"Have you ever ridden a horse?" Ellis asks, pulling the drink to her lips and drinking. I try not to watch her mouth part over the lip of the can, but ever since her little slip up about riding something, I've turned into some kind of horny teenager.

I wrap my arm around her shoulders and pull her in closer, the smell of jasmine wrapping around me. "As a kid, sure," I answer honestly. "But I'm pretty sure the horse was at least seventy years old, and he would have gone wherever the trail guide went. I'm not sure it counts." When she beams up at me, my chest tightens. She's just so fucking beautiful, even backed by dead animals and a ranch that's now full of people getting just a touch sloppy. "You?"

Ellis looks forward, watching as another rider gets thrown, and the line moves again. There's one more person before us.

"Same," she says. "One more to go."

Nerves start twisting my stomach in knots as the country music sounds through the large speakers by the stage. Guests have taken to the dance floor, throwing any formal swing dancing out the window and resorting to something far more similar to what you'd find in a city bar—though the belt buckles are far bigger.

Another rider falls, and Josh gestures to Ellis, encouraging her to climb over thick blue mats and onto the giant chunk of metal at the center.

She climbs onto the mechanical bull, adjusts the cowboy hat on her head, and offers me a megawatt smile that does something funny to my insides.

I'm so down bad.

Noah and Ryan are going to love it.

"You ready there, Miss?" Josh calls through his small microphone, and Ellis nods in his direction, grasping the rope with one hand and holding her hat on with the other. Her dark hair spills around the oversized flannel she's wearing, her jeans tight in a way that I'm trying and failing not to notice. It's when I see the joy shining in her eyes, I realize I've somehow won the jackpot.

"Eight seconds, Miss," Josh says. "Yee-haw."

The bull starts slow. Nervous laughter pours through her lips as her hand tightens on the rope tied around the barrel. I cup my arms around my mouth, shouting to cheer her on. When I whistle loud enough for the entire ranch to hear, Ellis laughs.

The bull picks up pace, and I look at the timer stationed next to Josh. Three seconds.

"Halfway," I shout, a grin breaking across my face as the bull picks up speed. Ellis is tossing her head back laughing, legs clinging for dear life as her butt slides around the barrel. The timer sounds for eight seconds, and she hops off with a smug look on her face.

I hand back her drink as she pats me on the chest. Her cheeks are flushed, eyes glowing. "You're up next, Cowboy."

Josh waves me on. I hoist myself onto the fake animal, running a hand through my hair nervously and grabbing the rough rope. I'm pretty sure it's going to slice off my skin with how scratchy it is.

"Alright there, Bud," Josh starts. "I went easy on your lady there, but you and I both know you got more in you. One hand on the rope only. Eight seconds."

I swallow.

Fuck.

Country music blasts through the speakers. My palms are sweating, and my heart lodges in my throat. I think I black out.

One second I'm on the bull, and the next I'm on the mat, looking at the timer that reads two seconds. I lean my head back on the blue padding and stare at the ceiling.

Josh is laughing through the microphone, and I can hear Ellie's giggles from a mile away.

Pulling myself up, I allow myself to participate in a new kind of walk of shame, hopping down and feeling slightly better when Ellis draws me in for a hug.

Her bright eyes stare up at me, shining with unfathomable amounts of delight. "Not so bad."

"It was rigged." I can't help the smile on my face. My tone is void of any bite.

Ellis looks over to the bar where the same older woman is serving shredded chicken sandwiches and hot dogs.

"I'm starving," she announces. "Let's eat, and then can we dance?"

I take her hat off and plant a kiss on her temple before replacing it on her head. She could ask me anything, and I'd go along with her.

"Of course."

· · · · ● · ● · ● · · ·

"Ellie and Stuart?"

I nearly choke on my drink from where we're seated, turning to find a familiar blonde woman standing in a white skirt, flannel shirt, and pink cowboy boots.

"Oh god," Ellis whispers from the chair next to me. She throws back the rest of her second hard seltzer before turning to the woman behind us. "Cass?" she questions.

Cass smiles, closing her eyes and nodding as she realizes her mistake. "Sorry," she says. "It was so weird to run into you guys here. I heard what happened at the wedding. Can we try again? I'm Cassidy. Cass for short."

Ellis holds out her hand. "Ellis," she says with a wide smile. "And this is Griffin."

Cass tilts her head to the side, her blue eyes shining. "Griffin, huh?"

I chuckle as Ellis stands and leans to throw her can in the trash at the end of the table.

"Sorry about that," I say.

Cass points between us, one brow raised. "So, are you two actually married?"

Ellis giggles. "We actually met a few hours before the wedding."

"You're kidding!"

The two of them are laughing, and I stand up to take my place next to Ellie, wrapping an arm around her shoulders.

Cass notices the movement. "Well, it seems like that's working out." She takes a drink of the beer in her hand and pulls her phone out of the small tasseled bag hanging over her shoulder. "Look," she starts. "I actually just moved to Ohio a few months ago, and I'm looking for friends to hang out with. If you want, I can give you my number, and maybe we could hang out sometime."

Ellis grabs her unlocked phone and quickly types her number into Cass's contacts. She snaps a selfie of the two of us, sends it to herself, and hands back the phone. "That would actually be great."

Cass seems pleased at that. "Where's Chad?" I ask, wondering where her asshat billionaire boyfriend ran off to. A country Christmas party doesn't seem like the place he'd want to go to.

Ellis nudges me with her shoulder, and I catch the hint of *you shouldn't have asked* in her eyes before Cass responds.

"Actually, I broke up with him after the wedding." Her face scrunches as if she's fighting how uncomfortable talking about it is. "He kept hitting on other women."

"I'm so sorry," Ellie says, and by the warmth in her tone, I'm inclined to believe her.

"It's alright. Well, I'll let you guys get back to what you were doing. It was nice seeing you again."

Upon her retreat, she accidentally bumps into Wes, and I turn to face Ellis, smiling down at her beneath the string lights hovering above us on the ceiling. "You want to dance?" I ask, and before I register what's happening, she's dragging me onto the dance floor and throwing her arms around my neck.

"So," Ellie begins. "Come here often, Stuart?"

I lean down, nudging the side of her head with my nose. "Shut up," I mutter, but there's no heat behind the words.

The music shifts, and suddenly there are more bodies crowding the dance floor. A few women bring their drinks along with them, and I'm realizing that the ranch has become somewhat of a country nightclub.

Ellis pushes in closer, and it sends heat down my spine, warming my entire body.

Lost in a sea of people, we shut the world out. Ellis spins, turning to face away from me and grabbing my hands to place them firmly on her waist. When her body connects to mine, I bite back a groan.

Fuck. Fuck. Fuck.

"You're not such a bad dancer after all." She's taunting me, and I know it. Ellis presses in, and I try to think of anything to keep myself in check. She's certainly not respecting space, and I can't say I don't enjoy it.

I get the thought that if she let me, I'd absolutely respect the fuck out of her.

"I was only pretending I can't dance," I say, my fingers tightening on her waist as she leans back against my chest, her body rubbing against–everything.

Double Fuck.

I'm hard. And I'm pretty sure she knows it.

I try to create some distance, get myself under control, and guide her to face me again. She's still pressed close, but this way I can actually think about something decent.

"You look good in that hat," I say, and I don't miss the way she smiles, her cheeks now tinted pink.

Her flush deepens as she keeps her gaze away from me. "And you look good with purple hair." She finally meets my eyes again, and I can see the heat there. God, do I want it.

Her hand reaches up, thumb brushing across my jaw. "Very Y'all-ternative."

I chuckle, spinning her the way we learned during our swing dance lesson. We didn't quite get this far, but the woman asked for something romantic, and I'm going to give it to her.

Guiding her with my hands, I get her to tip back, keeping a firm grip around her waist and sliding one hand up her thigh, brushing it over her ass. It's everything I ever dreamed it would be, but I'm trying not to be weird about it.

My nose traces a line against her neck before I pull her back up to stand. "And you're very pretty," I say.

Ellis giggles, drawing closer with her arms around me. "Yeah?" she says, her voice now low.

I grab the hat from her head again. While it looks great, it's in my fucking way. Bending down, I get my lips an inch from hers, the scent of jasmine invading my lungs. I couldn't want her any more than I do right now, and we've only just started. "Absolutely devastating."

With one hand placed gently on her throat and the other gripping her waist, I draw her into a kiss.

When her mouth parts, I swear the entire earth stops spinning.

Just for us.

Twenty

Ellis

My boots kick the gravel outside of The Handlebar Ranch as we walk through the darkness to Finn's car.

His hand clasps mine, warm and inviting, as the wind whips around us and whistles through the trees. The air is significantly colder than when we'd arrived, and my attention locks on the muffled voices near the ranch by the only light around the parking lot. Two guests lean against the side of the building.

Wes tips his hat when he sees me, pulling a cigarette to his lips and taking a long drag.

"Maybe we weren't so bad after all," I say, and Finn chuckles.

With little light, he grabs his phone out of his jeans pocket and turns the flashlight on, shining it by our feet so we can see where we are walking, just out of view of the side of the ranch.

With the quiet night surrounding us, my worried brain settles. I can't help remembering the way Finn's fingers felt against my throat as we kissed on the dance floor. How did he even learn to do that? His skin burned beneath my touch when I brought my hands to his face, and it awakened something in me.

That feeling hasn't gone away.

I want him, and the logical part of my brain seems to be on vacation.

"Thanks," I whisper as we approach the Jeep. "For the birthday, the dancing. All of it."

Finn leans forward, crowding my space. He's still wearing a smile, and I begin to think that the RBF from the coffee shop wasn't the real Finn at all. "You liked the dancing?"

My cheeks flame like a million suns–the memory of his body against mine is still fresh.

Finn grabs the handle, opens the door and gestures for me to slide in, but I just stand there, staring at him like an idiot.

My stomach dips when I realize how blessedly empty and *dark* the parking lot seems to be.

He stares at me; the smile dropping from his lips to be replaced by something else. It's hard to make out what it is without any street lamps, but I decide to take my chances.

I toss my hat into the car and grab his shirt to drag him to me, pressing my lips firmly against his. Finn softens to the kiss, his hands coming to rest around the sides of my face, fingers in my hair.

It's not enough. I only just met the guy, and I can't get enough of him.

When we break apart, Finn keeps his face close. His chest heaves, and we both fight to catch our breath.

Resting his forehead against mine, he moves one hand to drag the pad of his thumb over my bottom lip. It takes everything in me not to moan with that one touch.

"I've been waiting to do that again," he whispers.

I look up, my breathing shallow. "I want you so bad, I don't even know what to do with myself."

His eyes flick between mine, one hand moving to my waist where I feel his fingers tighten. Finn's other hand stays on the side of my face, gentle and welcoming, like everything about him.

"What is it you want?" he asks, his voice lowered–huskier than it was a few moments ago. "Exactly?"

I grip one of his belt loops and gently pull him closer. When he groans, I'm left spiraling out of control. "Everything," I whisper, before crushing my mouth into his.

Finn takes that as his cue to let go of whatever restraint he had. He walks me back until I can feel the coolness of metal behind me. His mouth parts, and I feel his tongue trace over my lip. He bites gently, tugging at my mouth like he wants to devour me.

When he lifts his hand higher and his thumb brushes just beneath my breast, I gasp, arching to encourage him to take more.

It's the only thought in my head.

More. More. More.

And when Giffin whispers, "Yeah?" against my lips, I'm certain I said the word at least once out loud.

My fingers fumble with the buttons of his shirt, desperately trying to get closer to him as he moves his mouth to my neck. When he presses his hips into me, I can feel how hard he is under those damn jeans. While they make his ass look phenomenal, all I want is to take them off.

"It's fucking cold, Ellie. You can't undress me out here." His tongue flicks out over my skin, as I undo the last button, fisting the fabric of his T-shirt.

"Then I'm not sure what I'm supposed to do."

Finn pulls away, smiling.

I can hardly stand still as I watch him close the passenger door and open the back door to his car. "My seats go down," he mutters, fumbling with whatever buttons or levers are inside. I'm not really paying attention.

"Thank god."

When the backseat is free and clear, I crawl in. Finn follows after me and pulls the door closed. It's still cramped, but it's far better than the front seat.

My back's against the side as Finn crawls over me. There isn't enough space to get close, and I drop my head and chuckle, his hand rising to cup my cheek.

"Hi," he whispers.

My eyes meet his. "Hey."

When he guides me to lie back, we struggle with space until my legs are open, knees bent, and Finn nestles himself between them.

His mouth is suddenly on my lips, my neck, my collarbones above the tank top I'm wearing. He's far more demanding than I imagined. So sure of himself and what he's doing. It makes my desire even sharper.

Finn's tongue swirls over the skin just above the swell of my breast, and I arch up, demanding more. His eyes are on me as he nods for confirmation. I nod back, and he grabs my tank top and the cup of my bra, pulling them down as his mouth closes over my nipple.

I cry out, too turned on to be embarrassed as he groans. His hips rock into me, and I grab at the flannel, pulling it off his shoulders. I grab his T-shirt and toss it with the flannel.

"I didn't bring a condom," he admits.

"Well, fuck." My breathing is still heavy, desire pouring through me.

His mouth pulls up at the corner. "We could try something else?"

He rocks his hips into me again, and I can't help the noise that passes through my parted lips. "Anything," I pant.

Finn's fingers are at the button of my jeans, his hands dragging them down my thighs and pulling hard to get them off. My boots and pants are gone, my hands trailing over his chest and arms.

He brushes a thumb over my nipple, circling until I'm certain I'll combust. It's too much. My body is buzzing and needy, and I'm not sure what's come over me. The only thing I know is that when I'm with him, it feels like the entire world opens up. Everything becomes a possibility. Finn came in like a summer storm, leaving me in the street to smile up at the rain.

It makes me want to drown in him.

When his hand migrates lower, he kisses my stomach, continuing higher as his tongue flicks out over my skin. His hand sinks lower–lower still.

When he pulls my underwear to the side, I can feel the slide of his finger, and I'm suddenly aware of how drenched I am. No sense in being embarrassed now.

His thumb presses down on my clit, and I moan–loudly.

"You can't do that." He's chuckling, pushing two fingers inside me as his thumb draws slow circles where I need him most.

"I–" I can't finish the words. Not when he's kissing me again, his fingers pumping in time with the stroke of his thumb. "Fuck," I whisper.

Finn's lips are by my ear, his breath fanning over my neck and leaving a trail of goosebumps. I can feel myself winding tighter–climbing toward the release that I'm craving. "I think this is the most I've heard you curse."

Another kiss swallows my breathy chuckle. My hips start rocking, and I reach down to fumble with his belt, unbuttoning his jeans and sliding my hand beneath the waistband of his briefs. His skin is hot as I stroke him. Finn lets out a sound that has me craving more. It's a dark rumble that drags from somewhere deep in his chest, and I want him to do it again.

We're both panting, rocking into one another and desperate. His breaths are hot on my skin as my body keeps climbing. Everything is tensing up, and I know that I'm about to come in the backseat of this damn Jeep. My dignity is gone.

"You're close." It's not even a question and the fact that he said it like that has me near the peak. His voice sounds strained, so I quicken my hand and he tenses.

I nod, my eyes locking with his. His mouth is parted, full bottom lip hanging in a way that has me leaning up to drag it between my teeth. He hisses, and his motions quicken.

"Keep riding my hand," he whispers. "I want you to come."

When he groans again, and I feel his body tensing, my orgasm rips through me. Pleasure takes over, and Finn kisses me through it as I feel his own release through my fingers.

His head falls to the crook of my neck, and I keep my eyes fixed on the roof, trying to catch my breath.

Glancing over at the windows, I laugh. "It's very foggy in here."

Finn's laugh vibrates over my skin–a sound that I want to keep and store with all the smiles I've collected. "You think?"

When he pulls away. He places one more rough kiss on my mouth before handing me my jeans and crawling over the center console to the glove compartment where he fishes out a pack of tissues.

"This is all I have," he says, his cheeks tinted pink in the dim lighting. "I don't usually–"

He doesn't finish the sentence, but I know what he means. "Me neither," I say, grabbing the tissues and cleaning up. We both begin pulling our clothes back on. "What are we? Like sixteen?" I say, realizing I just gave this man a handjob in the back of his Jeep.

I'll have the decency to be embarrassed when I confess to Lennon tomorrow.

Finn laughs again, using the keys to start the car. "That was far better than anything I did at sixteen," he says.

And I think I agree with him.

Twenty-One

Griffin

I wipe my hand down my face, staring at the screen for the second hour. Somehow, even when I have a good relationship with the band I'm mixing for, I still get nervous working on the project. This band, in particular, has provided fairly consistent work for me over the past few years.

What's even better is that I actually love their music.

I grab my coffee off the desk and take a swig of the lukewarm liquid before glancing at the clock. It's still before noon, the memories of yesterday still floating around in my mind.

I smile against the cup, thinking about the feel of Ellie's lips on mine and the flush of her skin beneath my fingers.

Fuck.

I slide my phone out of my pocket and dial Ryland's number. He picks up almost immediately.

"Hey man, I'm almost done mixing this track. It's fucking fantastic."

He chuckles, and I can hear some shuffling on the other end of the line. "Prompt as always," he says. "You never fail us, Griffin."

Something about it brings a smile to my lips. It's when I get to work for bands I enjoy that I remember why I wanted to do all this in the first place. Ryland's band, Elephant University, is one that always reminds me how music should sound, and I take pride in working on the tracks they put out.

"Hey, so listen," he begins. "We're opening for a bigger band early next year. The tour is short. We'll probably be on the road until the first few weeks of April. Anyway, they're looking for a new audio guy. Someone to mix front of house at the shows. Do you know a guy?"

I run my hand over the back of my head. "I don't know anyone off the top of my head who isn't already tied up." I clear my throat, my heart pounding in my chest, thinking about what Ryland's saying. "I mean, I've done sit downs and larger productions before. On the tech side of it I could do it, but I've never truly considered going on tour. I'm not sure I could make a decision that fast."

It's true. If they're looking for a guy, I could probably do it. My mom's words linger, etched into whatever wall I'd formed around the idea. My heart thrashes against my sternum, pounding an erratic rhythm as I think about it.

Could I leave my family?

Ellis?

I don't linger on the second thought. I haven't known her that long–its ridiculous.

"Oh sweet. Is that something you *might* consider? You know we'd love to have you. We love your stuff, obviously." Ryland's seriously asking me this.

I clear my throat again and question if it's weird I've done it twice now. I'm fucking nervous. It would be a cool opportunity, but I'm not sure I can commit with my job at the college. I'd have to quit to go on the road for a few months.

"I'm probably not the best option," I admit. "I've got that job at the college, and I'm not sure I'd be able to take the time. I could help you guys out in a pinch, but committing to something like that would take a lot of consideration."

For one, I'd lose my health insurance.

Though it would be so fucking cool.

"Yeah, that's alright. We'll keep looking. You said you're sending files over?"

I check everything on my monitor, clicking around before hitting send.

"Just did," I say. "Hope you guys like it."

Ryland's laugh breaks through the speaker of my phone. "Always do, man. Talk later."

I lean back in my chair, my eyes wide as I try to process the offer just thrown at me. It's not the first time someone offered me a gig, but something about this feels different. I've had a longstanding relationship with Ryland and his band. It might be cool to test out something new.

I hear the front door of my apartment open and spin around in my chair.

"Just me," Noah calls, and I grab my coffee to take another sip.

"I'm in the cave," I announce.

Noah walks through the closet door, throwing himself down on the beanbag in the corner. The same one Ellis sat in just under a week ago.

"What's that face for?" Noah asks, and I quickly school my features, shaking my head and turning to the monitor to pretend to do–*something*.

"Nothing," I mutter.

"Right." I can hear the smile in his voice. "So, how'd time with your girl go?"

I grab my phone, flipping to the freelance website to see if I can get any more jobs done before the end of winter break. "Not my girl," I say, though it doesn't feel true. I'm down so bad, I wouldn't be surprised if I pissed in a circle around her the next time another man glances in her direction.

"You never do anything halfway, Griffin. And honestly, it's not that often you're interested in a girl. You're like a serial monogamist or something."

I twist in my chair, hoping to sound as casual as possible. I don't feel like unloading all the shit that happened when my brother died. It's not something to relive. He's gone, it's fine. "I don't like to fuck around," I say, keeping my tone even.

"Yeah," he says. "I know."

When I turn to look at him, he pushes his glasses up his nose. Still wearing them, I guess.

Noah crosses his ankle over his knee, and I realize the guy is wearing dress pants. I shake my head and chuckle. "You're really holding to that dark academia aesthetic, aren't you?"

Noah's brow furrows. "It's working. I had a date yesterday."

My brows raise; my interest thoroughly peaked. "How'd that go?"

"Awful, but it doesn't matter." Noah waves a hand. "What about you and the girl? What are you guys doing?"

"Like dating?"

Noah looks at me like I'm an idiot. "Yeah, Griffin. Like dating."

I twist away from him, messing around on the monitor again. "I'm not sure, but I'd like to keep this thing going."

I can hear his judgment echoing through the room despite all the sound treatments I worked so hard to put up.

"You should ask her out," he responds. "Ask her out officially. Make it crystal clear."

"You think?" I ask, but I already know what his answer is. There's no reason to pretend I'm not going to do it. After last night, there's no way I couldn't. Not when my mind keeps circling back to every smile—every laugh that decorated her beautiful mouth.

Damn.

"Don't answer," I say, holding a hand up to stop him. A smile crosses Noah's face, and unfortunately, it's nowhere near as devastating as Ellie's. "I'm going to."

Noah reaches for the popcorn bag propped up on my desk and pops a piece into his mouth, his smile still firmly fixed on his face. "Good," he says.

Twenty-Two

Ellis

The Christmas tree farm is terribly picked over, and I'm certain Lennon and I are about to end up with a small stick instead of an actual tree.

"This was a terrible idea so close to Christmas," I say as we walk through the mud and grass mixture on the farm. The field of tall trees stretches out before us–towering pines that make me realize just how big the world is–how big it's felt since I met Griffin.

Unfortunately, *those* trees are not available to cut. We could, technically, but then we'd be paying a ridiculous amount per foot. While my marketing job pays enough, I don't make enough to go breaking the rules.

Lennon halts, giving me a flat look. Her red braid hangs over her shoulder, only restrained in the wind by the winter hat on her head. "Ellie," she says, clearly annoyed. "We go this close to Christmas every year, and it's always the same. It's literally been our tradition since college."

I chuckle, shoving my hands in the pocket of my coat as the breeze whips through the farm, carrying strands of my hair with it. I start to wish I'd chosen a winter hat instead of a winter headband instead. It might rein in my hair a bit more.

"I guess you're right, but it doesn't help that I had to work today. We're showing up an hour before closing, and I swear the workers were giving us dirty looks."

"You're just overly sensitive," Lennon states before holding up the handsaw she's carrying. "They can't give us dirty looks. We have a weapon." There's a pause—a brief moment that sends my mind drifting back to the car and the feel of Griffin's—

"Ellie?"

I turn to Lennon, a flush painting my cheeks pink. Hopefully she thinks it's from the cold, but somehow I doubt it. Lennon's been around a while. She can read my reactions well.

"What?" I say.

"First of all," she starts, pointing the saw at me. I step away. "If you're reliving what you told me you did with Finn yesterday, stop. That's a private thing I want no part of." I laugh. "Second of all, how are you feeling about your job now that it's been a few days?"

"I couldn't focus at all," I complain.

Lennon doesn't let me finish. "I can see why, and you better get that under control. You're no better than a horny teenager."

The flush on my cheeks turns a deeper shade of red. "Rupert thinks I've lost my mind. I may have confided in him about being unhappy."

"Well," she starts. "Have you? Lost your mind, I mean."

I mull over her words for a moment. "I don't think so."

The next thing she says surprises me. "I don't think so either."

I give Lennon a questioning look, pausing our walk to face her and waiting for whatever wisdom she has to offer.

"Listen," she starts. "You know I'd be the first person to tell you if you'd lost your damn mind." She cocks an eyebrow. "And honestly, I don't think you have this time."

It's my turn to deadpan. "Lennon, I let him–" I restart. "I rode his hand in the back of a Jeep."

Her laugh is light, eyes sparkling with mischief. "Sounds like fun, not insanity." Lennon steps forward, dropping the saw to the damp earth below and placing her hands on my shoulders. "You deserve to loosen up a little, Ellis. You're way too hard on yourself, and always concerned about how your existence is going to impact the people surrounding you." Her face scrunches up. "It's very annoying, but I already like you, so I can't say anything about it."

I chuckle. "You just did."

One eyebrow lifts, and it almost makes me feel like she's about to scold me. "Well, I can't very well ghost you at this point."

Lennon smiles and lets go of my shoulders as we continue walking. My phone vibrates in my pocket, and I quickly whip it out, taking one glove off to view the text.

Finn: *I need to see you again.*

I smile, and for some odd reason, Lennon doesn't interrupt.

Me: *When?*
Finn: *Now.*
Me: *I'm with Lennon. We're getting a Christmas tree.*

I look up at Lennon, and she makes a face that encourages me to continue. I don't question it as the bubbles pop up, and then I receive a response.

Finn: *Okay. Tomorrow.*
Me: *Working*
Finn: *Saturday?*
Me: *Okay.*
Finn: *Can't wait.*

When I finally glance up, Lennon is staring at a lopsided tree that, to be honest, looks like it should be used as firewood.

"That's the one," she says, prowling forward with her saw in hand.

I smile, pocketing my phone and pulling my glove back on. "You're absolutely right."

• • • ● • ● • ● • • •

I texted Cass after the Christmas tree farm, asking her how far she lived, and inviting her to watch cheesy Christmas romance movies with us. It didn't take long to receive a response, and luckily, she and Lennon got along extremely well.

They wasted no time. Starting the conversation strong with Cass bitching about Chad, and Lennon joining in despite not knowing the guy. I can't say he didn't deserve it. He turned out to be everything I thought he was.

"Thank you guys for inviting me," Cass says from her spot, curled up on the couch. She sips her hot chocolate, quickly wiping the whipped cream off her upper lip.

We all wore sweatpants, which was a phenomenal idea because we ended up watching three movies in a row.

Lennon cried for two of them, but she'd never tell you that.

"I'm actually glad you showed up," I say, and I mean it.

"I'm her only friend," Lennon announces, and I throw a pillow in her direction. She's still laughing and undeterred. "Ellis has too much anxiety to hang out with other people. Thank God you're friendly. I can't be the only one to bear the burden of friendship."

I'm laughing now. "You're literally so mean."

"Yes," she says, a smile firmly fixed on her face. "I am."

Cass is laughing too when a knock sounds at the door. My brow furrows, and I slowly stand up, considering grabbing the largest book I own for protection.

"Who would knock on your door this late?" Cass asks.

Lennon's smile falls, sarcasm dripping from her lips. "We're about to get murdered."

I shake my head, opening the door and gasping when a very tall, and very familiar man greets me at the door.

"What are you doing here?" My voice sounds breathless, and I know Lennon is practically jumping out of her chair behind me.

Finn holds up a grocery bag filled with popcorn and other snacks. "I'm not staying," he says. "I brought this, though." I take the bag from him. "There was just something I wanted to ask you."

I'm whisper yelling, but there's no bite to my tone—not when I can't stop grinning from ear-to-ear. "You couldn't have just texted me?"

Finn rubs the back of his neck nervously, his cheeks flushing beneath my porch light. "It felt important?"

He shrugs, and I find my gaze dropping briefly to his mouth. By his smug smirk, he seems to notice it.

"Hey, Finn," Lennon says from her spot on the couch, inserting herself in the conversation.

Finn waves and spots Cass on the couch. He gives me a questioning look, and I shrug.

"Good to see you, Cass," he says.

I chuckle, closing the door behind me and moving to the porch with him for some privacy. For a moment, I think I hear a noise on the other side of the door—Lennon eavesdropping, no doubt.

"I want to take you out." His voice comes out in a rush. "Not for your birthday." He's nervously fumbling over his words, and I can't help how it warms my chest. "I want to take you out on dates, Ellie. Real ones. I don't want to go back to being strangers, and I sure as shit don't have any interest in anyone else."

My cheeks are flaming despite the cold air outside. I can barely look at him. This is the stuff for the movies.

"Is it a yes?" he asks, his voice still breathless.

When I look up at him, I can't help but see the hope in his eyes. I stretch up, planting a kiss on the corner of his mouth before dropping back down. "It's a yes, Griffin."

"Finn," he corrects.

I nod, wrapping my arms around myself to fight off the cold. "Finn," I say. "It's obviously a yes."

He pulls me in for a kiss before spinning on his heel and walking down the porch steps to his car, turning back no less than three times before getting in the Jeep.

Once he drives off, I open the door to find Lennon standing directly on the other side.

Cass is with her, and they both have the most amused expressions.

"That boy is down so fucking bad," Lennon says, her eyes glittering in the living room light.

Cass giggles, tilting her head to one side. "Are you sure you guys just met?"

I pick up the bag of snacks and close the door behind me. "I'm sure."

Twenty-Three

Griffin

The gray sky stretches over the city as I drive through the streets. Snow flurries had started to fall to the ground, but any trace of the magic quickly dissolved into the earth. It's the kind of snow that keeps the roads easy to drive, and the hope for a white Christmas in the air.

As I round the corner, I pull into Ellie's driveway and throw the car into park.

Sliding out of my seat, I move to stand, close the door, and nervously push the sleeves of my brown, crew neck sweater up to my elbows. I immediately regret that decision when the cold air bites at my skin, and I pull the sleeves back down. If Ellie is watching me from the window, I'm certain I look like an idiot.

Walking up to the porch steps, I lift my hand to knock, but the door opens before I get there. Ellie's wide smile greets me, and I open the screen door to let her out.

"Are we leaving right now?" she asks.

"I mean, we can leave whenever. It's our date. Why?"

She grabs my arm, dragging me into the living room and closing the door behind me. "Stay right here. I'll be right back, and I don't want you to wait out in the cold."

I'm left standing alone to take in the dark green walls and the collection of photographs hanging by the door. I see Ellie with a woman who looks similar to her, a tall man, and a small child no more than two-years-old. There's another photo, too. One that makes an ache form in the middle of my chest.

Ellie looks eight or nine. Both front teeth are missing, and she's smiling up at the sun through the trees. Knelt down next to her is another woman with the same soft brown eyes, her hair braided over one shoulder–her mouth firmly planted on Ellie's cheek. The bottom corner of the photograph has some scribbled handwriting.

Mom and me. Before.

"Before the cancer." I turn to find she's returned, a steaming travel mug gripped in one hand. Her long dark hair partially tucked into her puffy coat.

I don't say anything–knowing exactly how she may feel in this moment. I know that when my brother died, I loved talking about the good memories. It helped me cope. But people were far more curious about the crash—the thing that killed him. Days were filled with *I'm so sorry,* and *how did it happen?* The worst was when they would inevitably ask if he was drunk.

He wasn't.

I stay silent, waiting to see what Ellie wants to share instead of asking. To me, it's the kindest thing I can do.

"I have a lot of memories with her," she begins. "That one's my favorite, though." Ellis sets her coffee mug on the end table and walks over to me to stare at the picture. I'm not sure what to do, but I want to do something. Without looking, I move my hand just slightly, but it doesn't matter. She wraps her pinky around mine as we stare at the person who was taken from her.

I hate that it happened at all.

I hate that we both know what it's fucking like.

"She used to take me to the nature centers in all the surrounding parks. I think it's because it was free, and being a single mom, free was always the best option." When I look at Ellis, her eyes look glassy. "I like this picture because she's kissing my cheek, and she looks really happy about it, too." I can't imagine anyone who wouldn't be happy about being around Ellis. She's bright like the stars. A steady light—one that brings peace to the darkness.

"You said your aunt raised you?" I ask.

"Yeah, B. She's great, but I know it was hard on her. It's not easy to graduate college and suddenly have a dead sister, and a thir-teen-year-old you have to take care of." Ellie looks over at me. "Sorry. We aren't supposed to be talking about this."

"I like that you are," I say, my voice low. "Talk as much or as little as you like. I want to hear what you have to say. I want to know you, Ellis."

She offers me a small smile. "Ready?" she asks.

Grabbing her hand, I squeeze once before picking up her coffee mug and holding it. "Yeah."

When we get into the Jeep, I start the car and find her hand again. For whatever reason, I don't want to let go. I wouldn't drop her fucking hand for anything.

"Where are we going?" she asks.

I smile at her. "You said you wanted to sleep under the stars on your bucket list. It's December, cold as shit, and a little too early for sleeping."

"Okay," she drags out the word, her brows furrowing.

I steal a kiss before letting my foot off the brake, and pulling away from her house.

"We're going to the science museum, Ellis. They have a planetarium. It was the best I could do."

Ellis leans over the center of the Jeep, resting her head on my shoulder. "It's perfect," she says.

• • • • • • • • • •

After we arrived at the planetarium, the tone shifted, and I found myself unable to wipe the grin off my face. I'm not sure I know anything about the stars, though.

I couldn't stop watching Ellie's full mouth, feeling the way she squirmed whenever I'd gently squeeze her thigh in the darkened room. It brought back the memories from the ranch. I couldn't get close enough.

Driving back to the house, I glance over to the passenger seat. There's no way I'm ready for the day to end–no way I'm ready to stop being with her.

Noah was fucking right, and I both hate him and love him for it.

"So," I start, hoping that she won't pull the handle and dive out of a moving vehicle when I ask her the next question. "It's Christmas Eve."

Smooth.

"I'm well aware," she says, giggling as she tips her head back against the seat and closes her eyes.

"I have to go to my parents tonight," I say, and her eyes open, widening when she looks at me.

Fuck. She's onto me.

"I'm not trying to freak you out." This is going about as well as I expected. "People make a big deal of meeting parents and shit. I just showed up at your door the other day asking you to go on a date, and now I'm saying this. I just thought it'd be fun, and your aunt's still on her cruise. I'm not sure if you and Lennon have plans, but—"

"Finn?" Her lips pull into a smile, and it brings a small amount of relief.

"What?"

Ellis pulls at her seatbelt, giving her the freedom to stretch over and plant a kiss on my cheek. When she's back in her seat, she has a satisfied grin on her face.

"What?" I ask again with more urgency.

"I don't have any plans," she says. "I'd love to hang out with your family."

Twenty-Four

Ellis

I started thinking about my mom. I thought about Lennon's words, Aunt B, the photograph hanging on my wall by the door, and the reason I put it there.

I didn't stop thinking, and for some reason, Finn didn't mind.

His fingers stayed laced through my own for the entire car ride, soft music playing from the radio. It seemed like maybe he knew what was going on, but I didn't want to be a burden. I didn't want to start talking because once I did, I'm pretty sure I wouldn't stop.

I glance out the window, watching as we start down a winding street, tall pines lining the steep hills running along one side of the road. Finn squeezes my hand again, and it quiets some of my thoughts.

"I'm not sure what's going on in your head," he says. "I just wanted you to know that I'm having the best time with you, Ellie." He squeezes again, and I look up at his face. His eyes glue themselves to the road, and his jaw ticks. "You got really quiet all of a sudden."

"I started thinking about my mom," I admit. I'm not sure why I said it, and I certainly don't know why I want to continue, but I do. "I've enjoyed being around you, too, Finn." The smile I offer him doesn't reach my eyes as much as I'd like, but I hope he knows I mean it. "Lennon thinks you're a good thing." The smile comes easier as Finn's gaze slides in my direction. "She said something about how I'm always concerned about how my existence is impacting the people around me, but I don't feel that way with you. You know how the summers here get insanely hot and humid? It makes you want to die from heat stroke if only to end the pain."

Finn's brows furrow. It's an expression so cute, my mood shifts a little more. "I guess," he says.

"Being with you is like that first fall day where the air is crisp again. It's like you can move and breathe without all the heat around you–the weight of the world, I guess." The song on the radio changes, and I find myself tapping along with a finger on my knee, finding my way back to the present.

"That's–"

I look at him. "Cheesy?" I offer.

"Really fucking nice."

It's not the answer I expected, and it makes me smile. I lean my head back on the seat, feeling more confident. "I felt like that with my mom, but then I watched B lose herself because of me. And even though my brain knows that she did it because she loves me and loved my mom." I keep my eyes closed, feeling the gentle curve of the road stretched out in front of us. "Loves my mom. She still loves her. Even though my brain knows that, I think my heart has always been scared to ask for too much. I don't want to be a burden, you know?"

When I finally open my eyes, Finn is looking at our joined hands. He squeezes one more time before focusing on driving, and for that, I'm thankful. I really can't die today. I'm just now figuring my shit out. And I am really, very happy.

"You're not a burden, Ellie." His hand tightens on the steering wheel as we round another curve. "You're wanted. And you don't have to be perfect for that to stay true."

I will not cry in this fucking Jeep. I cannot cry in the same Jeep I came in just days ago.

"I could see how much your mom loved you in that photo, and from what you told me, I think your aunt feels the same way. You needed her once. It's not like you're never allowed to need anyone again." Finn squeezes my hand again, and it starts to feel like a pulse–one that reminds me I'm still alive and breathing–still living this adventure with him. "When Storm died, my family was a fucking mess. I needed my mom and my sister more than I ever had before. It was embarrassing since I was a teenager, and obviously thought I had all my shit together. We're closer for it. You can let yourself lean on people. It's hard, but just know that you can."

For the first time since we started talking on this ride, I squeezed his hand back. "Thanks," I say.

"For telling you the truth?"

My smile widens, my chest swelling with the past few weeks. I can't believe he's real. "For being terrible at swing dancing," I say.

When Finn laughs, I drink in the sound. "Oh, my darling, Ellie," he starts. "I was the star of the class."

· · · · ● · ● · ● · ● · ·

My stomach decides to do weird flips and turns as we walk through the door of Finn's parents' house. It's basically an acrobat, and I'm one Cirque Du Soleil move away from throwing up on the concrete.

Finn calls out when we walk through the door and onto the landing, taking off our shoes before climbing the small set of stairs to the upper level. When we enter the living room, my eyes track to the tall woman on the couch. Her black hair glances just off her shoulders, and she wears a nose ring.

"Hey, Shitface." She hurls a pillow at Finn, and he quickly deflects it.

When he picks it up off the floor, he returns the favor. "I haven't seen you in three months, and this is how you greet me?" he says, but they're both smiling widely.

"Skylar," a woman's voice cuts through the air from what I assume to be the kitchen. When she strolls out, I instantly know who she is. Finn's mom wipes her hands with a rag and tosses it at the girl on the couch. "Show some respect. We have a guest in the house."

When she turns to me, I hear Skylar's soft laugh just beneath the sound of music floating in the air.

"Ellis," Finn's mom says, drawing me into a warm hug. "I'm so happy to finally meet the woman who inspired my son to come to the house for an extra visit in search of flannels and cowboy hats."

She lets go, her hands still gently grasping my shoulders.

"It was very fun. Thanks for letting us borrow the shirts."

Skylar chokes on air as another girl, shorter with auburn hair braided down her back, walks into the room. "Wait," Skylar says, nearly laughing. "You made your girlfriend wear *dad's* shirt?"

"Oh, Griffin." the new girl says before throwing herself on the couch and draping her legs over Skylars.

When I turn back to Finn, his cheeks are pink. He gestures to the couch. "Skylar and her partner, Brooke," he says.

Finn's dad walks in, quickly introducing himself and wrapping his wife in his arms. He twirls her around the living room as everyone else chuckles–including me.

There's so much warmth cluttered in every corner of the house, like the eccentric items stuffed wherever anyone could reach.

I love it.

"So," Finn's dad begins from his dance near the fireplace. "What is it you do, Ellis?"

I clasp my hands in front of me, trying to settle my nerves. "I work in marketing."

"She also draws," Finn quickly adds. "Her sketches are fantastic." He smiles at me, and I commit it to memory, just like all the others.

His parents stop dancing. "Oh my God!" his mom says. "You have to see the sunroom." She's grabbing my hand, dragging me down the hall to the back of the house. "I was *just* working on this painting, and I have plenty of art supplies." Finn shrugs when I look back at him, the light in his eyes letting me know he is not going to save me. "We can chat and get to know one another."

Finn calls from behind us. "Mom, that might be too intense."

I smile when she stops, looking into my eyes with so much hope it's like staring into the sun. "I think I'd like that," I say.

• • • • ● • ◗ • ● • ● • •

Finn followed us into the sunroom, but quickly left when we both found our seats and got to work. It felt good to sketch, and it felt good to talk to Finn's mom.

After the conversation in the car, it was like the universe placed me in just the right moment–in the presence of a woman I desperately needed, even if I didn't know it, yet. Everything about his family was like that.

They were easy to talk to, and so clearly loved one another. It's the kind of love you try to run from, and simply cannot escape–the thing churches spend so much time preaching about.

"That's beautiful." June Peterson looms over me, staring at the picture of a forest of pines.

"You think?" I say, turning back to see the look on her face. You'd think she was looking at real art.

After asking, Finn's mom picks it up, her eyes sweeping over the scene. "Absolutely stunning," she says. "I'm surprised you haven't done something with this talent. You're into marketing?"

"Well, yes," I answer. "Though it's not my favorite. It's a job, though."

When she sets the sketch down, she continues. "My paintings are going to be featured in an art show around the end of March. If you'd like, I'd love to throw some of your drawings in there. We can see how they do?"

My heart beats faster. "Really?"

Finn's mom squeezes my shoulder. "Of course, dear. You work on them, and we will make it happen." She leans down like she's telling a secret. "They like me too much to tell me no, anyhow."

Our attention shifts when Griffin appears at the door. "Dad said food's here." I offer him a little wave, and he rolls his tongue along his cheek, his eyes lighted.

"Delivered?" I ask, if only because it's Christmas Eve.

When I stand up, Finn's mom chimes in. "I can't cook to save my life," she admits. "We ordered from one of the few restaurants open. I hope you don't mind."

"Of course not."

When I walk out of the sunroom, Finn takes my hand in his, and for the rest of the evening I find myself lost in the festivities, and the people who helped him become exactly who he is.

Kind.

Twenty-Five

Griffin

S now falls gently over Ellie's house, floating down just in time for the holiday, and I can't help but think the day has been perfect.

Hell, the last few weeks have been perfect.

I walk up the concrete steps and pause by the door, thankful that Ellie hasn't withdrawn again.

To be honest, I didn't know what to fucking do, but I knew something was up in the car. Usually when we're together, we spend the entire time talking, so the radio silence worried me.

I'm glad she talked to me though–that she felt I was worth opening up to. And the way she interacted with my family?

Fuck.

If I was down bad before, I'm now a complete goner for this girl.

I brush a strand of hair behind her ear, the cold wind swirling around us, but I don't care.

"I had a lot of fun on our date," she says, and damn if it doesn't warm my chest right through. The snow doesn't exist anymore. There's only her.

"Yeah?" I ask, my fingers still running along her cheek. I don't want to leave yet.

"Yeah. I like your family, too."

I smile before leaning down to brush my lips over hers. It's not like the other night. It's soft and warm. The kind of kiss that feels real. Like it means something.

When I pull away, I keep my lips close to hers. "Goodnight, Ellie." Turning on my heel, I make the walk back to the Jeep, but before I get halfway there, her voice halts me.

"Do you want to come inside?"

I try to turn around slowly–try to keep myself from running back to her because it would be fucking weird. Instead, one corner of my mouth turns up, and I mutter, "sure." It's the understatement of the century.

When we get into the house, Ellis guides me through the living room and back to the kitchen. I hook my foot around the leg of the barstool next to her countertop and pull it out far enough to sit.

Placing the leftovers in the fridge, Ellis busies herself as I take in the spice rack by the window above the sink and the candle placed in the middle of the stove.

"Is that a fire hazard?"

Her head pops up from the other side of the refrigerator door and her brown eyes glance toward the whiskey and oak labeled jar of wax.

"I have home insurance," she answers, drawing a breathy chuckle from my lips.

Ellie closes the fridge, moving toward me, and I spin on the stool to face her. She plants herself in between my legs—the same way she stood in my bathroom the first time we kissed. Something about the position has my nerves firing in the wrong way, creating sparks across my skin. Especially when I place my hands on her hips and draw her closer.

"When's our next date, Finn?" she asks, wrapping her arms around my neck and pressing closer. I can feel the heat of her body—see the golden flecks in her eyes in the moonlight spilling in from the window.

I want to touch her.

I need her closer.

I lean down, running my nose along her neck until my lips are hovering an inch away from her ear. When her body shivers, I know she feels it, too. Everything tightens, and I'm left thinking about the way her body rocked into my hand—the sounds she made when she finally broke apart.

"Whenever," I whisper, my voice barely a rasp as I trail my lips over her flushed skin.

Ellie tilts her head to the side to give me better access, and I slowly work my way back up before nipping at her ear. The soft whimper has my cock straining against my pants.

Her hand is in my hair, tugging at the roots as I dip my head lower, peppering kisses over her shirt until I can barely take it anymore. My hands fist the hem, and I drag it up over her head, her black bra pulling a groan from some animalistic part of me I didn't know existed.

"Fuck, Ellie," I whisper. "You're breathtaking."

Her grip on my hair tightens when my mouth moves to her breast, my hand firmly grasping the cup of her bra and pulling down. I swirl my thumb over her nipple before taking it in my mouth, flicking my tongue over the hardened peak until I can feel her breaths pouring out fast and hard.

"Tell me you brought a condom this time," she breathes, and I smile against her skin.

"Maybe."

"Finn," her tone is a warning.

Standing, I move my hands down, grabbing her thighs and lifting her off the floor. I hold her tightly as her lips crash into mine, tongue exploring and fingers squeezing my shoulders.

"I won't drop you," I chuckle, walking through the living room and back to the hallway.

"First door on the right."

Her voice is shaking, and something about that sends pleasure shooting down my spine. I want to make this girl writhe beneath me. I want to feel her around my cock. I want it all.

When I stumble into her bedroom, I set her down on the bed and notice the heat in her eyes.

Ellie's ripping at the buttons of her jeans, frantically pulling them down and tossing them to the floor.

There's nothing I can do but watch, my chest rising and falling faster as I'm blessed with the view of more skin–more of her.

"Well," she says. "Are you going to help me or not, Griffin?"

I grunt, pulling my own jeans off–my briefs along with them. "Finn," I correct, and she laughs.

"Take my bra off, Finn. It's way too tight." The look on her face is devious, and I want to kiss her so fucking bad.

When she arches up, I undo the clasps, and move to take her underwear off, drinking in every inch of flushed skin when I'm hovering above her. "Stop making demands," I say, offering her a smug smirk.

Ellie leans up, kissing the corner of my mouth. "Get on your back," she says before I feel her hand in my hair again. I groan when she tugs my head back, placing a kiss on my neck. "Please," she whispers.

"Well, fuck."

Without thinking, I move, and suddenly she's over me, trailing kisses down my tensing stomach as my mind catches up with my body. Her hair spills over her shoulders, her lips swollen, and when her hand slides over my hardened flesh, I hiss.

"I can't take my eyes off you," I admit as her tongue flicks out, sending heat everywhere.

"Then don't."

Ellie's mouth parts around me, and I'm suddenly fighting the urge to thrust, trying to calm my rapid heartbeat as pleasure rips through my body, tightening my skin and making it hard to breathe.

Her hand works in time with her lips–her tongue, and I begin to realize my love for monogamy and meaningful relationships has left me ridiculously out of practice.

"Ellie," I gasp, but I don't think she hears me. "Ellis."

"Hmm?" The sounds she makes vibrates over my skin and fuck. *Fuck.*

"Ellie, slow down."

When she pulls away, her eyes blazing, I find the strength to bring myself back down. I was so close–too fucking close.

Flipping her over, I hold both of her wrists above her head, my tongue dragging over the swell of her breasts, swirling around her nipple. She arches into me, and I trail my mouth back up her chest and throat to swallow the noises breaking free from her lips.

"My turn," I whisper before dragging that full bottom lip between my teeth. "Stay here."

I lean over and fish the condom out of my pocket, tearing the packet open with my teeth before sliding it on. When her legs wrap around my waist, I almost lose my damn mind.

"You're sure?" I ask. "Because once I start this, Ellie, it's going to be really fucking hard to stop."

She reaches down and runs her fingers over me, a small smile ghosting over her lips. "I've never been more sure."

My mouth is on hers as I rock my hips forward, sliding into her slowly until I'm fully sheathed.

Her nails scratch at the skin on my back, and I'm suddenly lost, thrusting in time with my heartbeat, pulling sounds from her throat and trying to last as long as humanly possible.

It's no easy task.

Not with how fucking beautiful she is.

"More," she whispers, and it's the same word she said against my car. I'm powerless.

My movements become faster, pleasure spiraling until all I'm thinking about is slick skin and the harsh breaths sounding through her bedroom. My thumb finds her clit, and she moans, her breaths becoming more labored in a way that drives me forward.

It's all heat until my gaze catches hers. With her mouth parted, her eyes shining, I can't look away. I allow the build to rise, swelling until I can feel her everywhere–all around me.

"Are you close?" she asks, and I watch the way her brows pinch together.

"Yeah."

Her body is tightening, and I lose all grip on reality–my orgasm pulsing through me as she cries out.

When her breathing slows, and I move, allowing her to rest her head on my chest, she tightens her grip on my waist.

"I'm really glad I hired you, Finn."

I chuckle, running my fingers through her hair.

"I'm really glad you did, too."

Twenty-Six

Ellis

A heavy weight hangs over my waist when my eyes crack open. The gray light streams in from the window as I feel Finn shift behind me.

He curled his body around mine, encasing me in heat and memories from the night before.

I can still feel his hand in my hair, the way his tongue felt on my lips–all of it.

When he shifts behind me, I turn toward him, taking a moment to drink in the dark purple hair, the soft stretch of his mouth, the way I don't know how I ever thought this man could look mean. It makes me want to punch past Ellis in the face.

"Hey," he whispers, his grip tightening around me and sending heat to my cheeks.

"Merry Christmas," I say, and he chuckles, nuzzling into my hair.

"Right," he says. "I'm due back to my parents' around one."

I stroke my thumb over his hand before gently removing his arm. I desperately wish I didn't need to. "Lennon will be here this morning," I say, and his eyes finally open. "Don't worry." I glance at the clock on my nightstand. "We've got an hour and a half, but I need to get ready."

"Okay." Finn brushes a kiss across my cheek before rolling over onto his stomach.

When I get out of the bed, I allow myself to look back one more time, smiling before I enter the bathroom, peel my clothes off, and start the hot water.

The steam fills the room as I step in, but it only takes moments for the door to creek open. For the first time since living alone, I don't think the random sound is a serial killer.

Finn's never been a Ted Bundy kind of guy, anyway.

"Can I join you?" His deep voice sends goosebumps over my skin despite the temperature of the water.

I poke my head out from behind the curtain. "Depends," I say. "How hot do you like your showers?"

When he smiles, my chest aches. "With you in them?" he begins. "Absolutely scorching."

I smile back. "Perfect."

Finn almost seems too big for my shower. His head stops just above the showerhead, so he has to duck under to get beneath the spray.

A strand of damp hair hangs in front of his forehead, dripping as he grins. "You need help?" he asks.

My heart stutters in my chest, my stomach suddenly tightening, and my body buzzing with the memory of his skin on mine. "With?"

Finn cocks a brow. "Soap."

I fight the urge to look down and simply nod, turning away from him when he grabs the bottle from the ledge and gathers some in his hands.

He starts slowly, two fingers sliding up my spine, wet with the water droplets on our skin. When his lips meet my shoulder, I moan, tilting my head to the side and forgetting my own damn name.

"I haven't even started," he whispers as his hand wraps around my waist and lowers to my hip. His fingers tighten when he pulls me back to him, and I can feel how hard he is already. "Where should I begin, Ellie?"

Oh god.

I'm panting. My mind is dizzy with lust when I feel his hand brush soap over my ribcage. "Here?" he asks, before slowly dragging his palm lower.

The tension is winding tighter. I'm trying to keep myself upright. My knees weaken. When his fingers dip just above where I need him, he stops, starting the slow trek back up my body. It's a heady kind of torture. His thumb flicks over my nipple, palm still dragging soap over my skin. I gasp. "Oh, fuck."

He chuckles, and the sound vibrates against my skin. Finn kisses my shoulder, my neck. "Such a dirty mouth when you're so turned on," he says.

I feel his tongue trace over the side of my throat, cool compared to the temperature of the water. His hands are moving now, dragging over my body to cover my skin. Water droplets drip from that loose strand of hair at his brow, and land on my chest, sliding down between my breasts.

When I finally rinse off the soap, Finn is still looming close behind me. I can't think about anything but him. I want him inside me again.

"Condom," I whisper.

"On the sink outside of the curtain." His answer doesn't bring me the relief I crave, but it's enough. "I'd like to do something first."

He gently guides me to turn around, pressing until my back is against the shower wall. Finn slowly runs his hand over the outside of my thigh. He grasps just above my knee to lift my leg and places my foot on the lip of the tub. I'm entirely bare to him. Then Finn does something that has me letting go of all rational thought.

He drops to his knees, his firm hands holding me open. When he stares up at me, my heart thrashes in my chest. The water drips around his face, down his torso to the hair blazing a trail on his lower stomach. When I nod in confirmation, he leans forward, and I feel his hot breath just before his tongue.

"Fucking hell," I rasp.

Finn chuckles, slowly moving one hand until he presses two fingers inside of me. He's stroking, licking, keeping time better than anyone I know, and I'm suddenly thankful he considers music to be his passion.

"Finn." I can't stop. My hips move, rocking in a way that should be embarrassing, but when he groans, I throw the embarrassment right out the window. He presses in, sucking as the pleasure rips through me. I cry out, fisting my hand in his hair. His fingers continue stroking, his tongue slowly easing to a halt until my body stops trembling.

Before I have time to fully recover, he's up and reaching out of the shower to the sink. Once the condom is on, Finn spins me away from him, gently placing my hands on the shower walls. The water sprays around us, the steam creating a thick fog.

He places a gentle kiss on my neck, and it draws me back to the present. Finn's warm chest presses against my back, the weight of it maddening. "I don't want to stop going on adventures with you," he whispers so close, a shiver tumbles down my spine. "In case you were wondering."

When I speak, my voice is breathless. "I wasn't wondering that at all," I admit. My mind only preoccupied with the direct present. "But it's still nice to know."

Finn chuckles, and within moments, he's easing inside of me. I clench at the fullness, and press back into him. The noise he makes awakens some kind of feral beast inside me, and my back arches.

He's thrusting, and my fingers are pressing into the shower wall, my body suddenly climbing all over again.

When Finn moves a hand to where I need him most, he keeps time with his hips, drawing pleasure from every possible corner of my body. His grip tightens on my waist just before his thumb tilts me forward. Everything feels deeper and more intense. A dark sound drags from deep in his throat, sending me over the edge with him.

The water's gone lukewarm, but there's still so much steam in the room, it reminds me of the windows of his Jeep.

Finn's head falls to my shoulder, his wet hair sending droplets of water down my back. I can feel the deep rumble of his voice everywhere. "I can't get enough of you," he says, and I am certain I feel the exact same way about him.

• • • • ● • ● • ● • • •

Once dressed, I walk Finn to the front door, kissing him as his fingers gently brush against my throat, reminding me of everything we've done.

He keeps his lips close to mine. "Merry Christmas, Ellie."

I smile. "Merry Christmas," I whisper before letting him go.

When Finn opens the door, Lennon is standing on the other side with her fist raised as if she were just about to knock. Which is strange, but then I realize Finn's car is parked out front.

Her eyes are so wide, I swear they're about to pop out of her head. She must have realized who the car belonged to, but in this moment, doesn't seem to believe it's true.

Griffin nods, offering her a wide smile while adjusting his coat. "Good to see you, Lennon." He's walking past her, but I don't miss the glint in his eye when his gaze briefly flicks back to me. "And Merry Christmas."

For the first time in Lennon's life, she has nothing to say. Her mouth hangs open as she watches him climb into his car and drive down the road.

"Hey," I mutter, my cheeks flaming.

"Hey?" she asks. "I just watched that man walk out these damn doors at ten in the morning on Christmas day looking like he just received the best sex of his life, and all you have to say for yourself is fucking hey?" Her voice rose the closer she got to the end of that sentence, and I chuckle.

Lennon points an accusing finger in my direction. "Don't you fucking laugh," she says. "I want details. Right now. Santa and baby Jesus can wait. They get this day every fucking year."

When she plows through the door, I take one extra second to look down the street where Finn's car disappeared.

Maybe I should have opened with *how are you* instead.

Twenty-Seven

Griffin

Ryan's tattoo gun buzzes as the sharp sting of the needle begins to numb. I glance out the window, noting the warmer March air, and thankful that the worst of winter has ended.

Though, I have to admit, Ellie's presence in my life has changed my perspective on the season entirely. Ever since Christmas, we haven't been apart for more than a few days at a time, and it's hard to imagine anything about my life before her.

"So," Ryan starts. "What's this one for?"

I glance down as he works with the gun, shading one of the keys. I decided to get piano keys tattooed on in the free space on one of my thighs just this morning. Ryan, as always, made space in his schedule.

"Nothing crazy," I answer.

Ryan pauses, his dark eyes glancing up at me as he rolls the toothpick between his teeth. "You texted me at eight in the morning to ask about getting this. It seemed urgent, and now you're telling me you're just fucking around?" He chuckles, returning to his work. "Come on, Griffin. Let's hear it."

I huff a laugh, trying to keep my body still as I remember the email from last night. "Ryland's band asked me to tour with them," I confess. "Front of house mixing. Running the desk. They're in a pinch for the last few shows over the college's spring break, and since it doesn't cut into my schedule, I actually think I can make it work."

Ryan halts his tattooing, leaning back in his chair. "No shit," he says. "You talk to Ellis, yet?"

I run a hand down my face. I knew the question was coming. "They only asked late last night." It's a shit answer. "I wanted time to get my thoughts together before I told her."

Ryan lets out a low whistle, the judgment clear in his expression. "So, you got a tattoo before you even asked your girl?"

I shake my head, chuckling. "She's with Cass, anyway. Lennon gets back from Minnesota tomorrow just in time for the art show. I figured I'd talk to her when I see her tonight." I give him a pointed look. "Once I figure out how I feel about it."

"Well." Ryan taps a gloved finger on the tattoo gun still buzzing in his hand. "It's just a few weeks, right? Very end of the tour."

My chest tightens. This is the part that makes me nervous–the part that makes me question what it is I really want. I love mixing, and my job has given me the stable income and health insurance I need. Even so, music has always been a part of me. I'd be lying to say the thought of doing something bigger didn't pique my curiosity. "It could turn into something more," I admit.

By the way Ryland's email sounded, if all goes well, they may consider hiring me for future tours. It would take me away from my family–from Ellis.

Ryan nods in understanding. He's known me for a long time–knows how much I value home. Still, I can't help getting the sense that there's something he isn't saying.

"Just tell me." My tone is flat.

One corner of his mouth turns up at that. "Ever since your brother died, you planted roots and haven't left. I mean, sure, you moved thirty minutes away from your family." His leg starts bouncing. "Skylar up and moved to New York. It's fine if you like it here, but who knows? This may be something good. You've just never realized it until now."

"I'll be away from Ellie." My chest aches. To be honest, I'm nervous to talk to her. In the back of my mind, I know it's something I want to do. Especially if I'll be working with Ryland's band. I know those guys, and I can't think of any better way to start.

"She's a good girl," Ryan states. "And she fucking loves you, whether she's said it yet or not. I'm sure it'll be fine."

His words pull at some deep feeling inside me, so I glance at the tattoo gun, allowing the smile to stretch across my face. "I'm paying you to give me this tattoo, Ryan. Why are you wasting my hard-earned cash by making it take longer?"

He chuckles, and when the needle breaks my skin, I swear the pain feels sharper. "Shut up, you asshat," he mutters.

• • • ● ● • ● ● • • •

When I walk into Ellie's living room, she's sitting on the floor in shorts and a black crew-neck sweatshirt. She braided her hair down her back, but strands break free around her face as she focuses on the parchment surrounding her.

It's absolute chaos.

"They're all terrible." Ellis stands, her brow furrowed as she steps over her mess, drawing into my chest and sending warmth through my veins. Sometime in the last three months, Ellis Smalley started to feel like home.

"They're not," I say before planting a kiss to the side of her head. She melts into me further. "But I get this is part of your process, and I know that you're nervous." I smile, squeezing tighter, if only for a moment. "I'm sure everyone will want to buy your drawings."

She chuckles, her fingers grasping my T-shirt at my back. "It doesn't count if you're the one buying them, Finn." When she pulls away, I can see the way her features have softened—the tension easing through her shoulders. She still doesn't let go. "You're barred from making any purchases at this art show. I need to see if my shit actually sells."

"Your shit?" I say, my brows rising. "Don't insult the drawings," I whisper. "They can hear you."

Ellis swats at me, and I chuckle, tossing my bag by the door and throwing myself on the couch cushions.

When she moves to sit next to me, she spots the bandage on my thigh, noting the new tattoo. "What's this one for?" she asks. Her fingers run over the clear plastic as a soft smile spreads across her lips. It still cracks my chest wide open. She's everything.

"Ryan did it this morning." I sit up as the nerves start working their way through my body. I suddenly feel like I'm about to tell her I murdered Noah for clogging my toilet again, and I need help hiding the body. "So, listen."

"Uh oh."

I laugh. "It's not bad." I run my hand through my hair, still purple. For a while, I let my hair go back to its natural color, but the day Ellie announced she missed how it was, we went out and bought purple dye again. It was no question. If she likes it, I like it. I also like how she couldn't stop touching me when I hopped in the shower to rinse it out.

"Ryland asked me to go on tour with them for a couple weeks to mix front of house."

Ellis sits up, excitement bubbling around her. "Shut up, Finn!" She leans forward, throwing herself on top of me. I grab her hips, drinking in the soft touch of her lips, the smile she can't quite wipe away. When she leans back, her brown eyes are sparkling. "I'm not entirely sure what it means, but you have to do it! When would you leave?"

"The day after the art show," I say, and I can't hide my wince.

"Oof," she says, but she doesn't pull away. "You have to up and leave in like two days?"

My breath leaves in a whoosh. Relief crashes into me when I see that despite the news, Ellie still doesn't look less excited for me.

I glance down at the sweatshirt. For once, it's not one of mine. "Reading is reading?" I question, tugging at the fabric. I don't know what the hell it means.

Ellie smiles. "Lennon bought this from some website she found. The Nightstand Book, I think it was called. You know how she tried to write a book forever ago? Anyway, it doesn't matter."

Placing her hands on the side of my face, she presses closer. "It'll be good." She kisses my jaw, the scent of jasmine wrapping around me in the way that drives me crazy. I keep my hands at her waist, fighting the urge to move them lower. "You'll have fun," she says before moving her mouth to the corner of mine. "I'll miss you." Another kiss. "But I can still send you texts and call." When she draws my bottom lip between her teeth, I groan. "All sorts of fun text messages," she says, and I can already feel the way she's pressing further into me.

"Fun text messages?" I question.

Ellis moves her legs to either side of my hips, her other hand rising to cup my face. She's so fucking breathtaking, I'm certain my entire chest is about to explode. I'm not sure why I was nervous to talk to her about it in the first place.

"Fun text messages," she says, and I catch the heat in her eyes.

I give in, sliding my hands from her waist to her ass, then squeezing. "Yeah?"

Ellis nods, her mouth suddenly on mine, and I swear the temperature in the room rises with every brush of her skin.

When she presses down, a noise rumbles from the back of my throat. I almost forget what we were talking about when her body rocks over mine, creating friction that has me desperate to show her exactly how much I'll miss her when I'm gone.

Something nags at the back of my mind, and I slowly pull away. Her eyes meet mine, and I almost know what she'll say before the words even leave my lips.

"It might turn into something more," I say. "Like I might get an offer to go on more tours."

Ellis nods, and while I don't miss the sadness that flashes in her eyes, she still doesn't seem opposed to the idea. "Okay," she says. "Is that what you want?"

I nod, thankful I spent the morning with Ryan sorting through my thoughts. "I think so." It's the honest answer.

Ellie's mouth breaks into a wide smile, one that reminds me of all the light she's brought with her–the *something* about her that has me begging to bask in her presence. "We'll figure it out," she says. "But I'm in this, Finn. I'm not scared of a little dream chasing."

That *something* burns brighter, and as I stare into her eyes, a thought plows through me. It's the thing that's lurked in the background for months–the thing I've known for a while now. I love her.

I am in love with her.

"Now," she says, pulling herself off of me. "Help me pick the last drawing to send over to your mom's. We have an art show tomorrow."

Twenty-Eight

Ellis

Over the past few months, I've decided my opinion on popsicles and their purposes has entirely changed. For one, they are not a food reserved for self-pity. They have since presented themselves as a frozen treat fit for all occasions—including babysitting during an unplanned brunch before your very first art show.

Eloise sits near the television, watching a movie and practically falling asleep while doing so.

We spent the entire morning playing scary coffee shop where she insisted on taking my coffee order, but sometime before I finished describing my drink, Eloise turned into a monster. The good news is I got my cardio running from first a zombie, then a werewolf, then a dinosaur. The bad news is that I didn't actually get coffee out of the deal.

I bite off the last piece of the popsicle and throw the stick in the garbage. Lennon's supposed to get back from Minneapolis and meet me at B's before the art show, and I could not be more nervous. Ever since Finn told me about the opportunity to test out going on tour, I haven't been able to wrap my head around it.

I'm excited.

I know how it feels to get to try out something you've been dreaming about. It's how I feel regarding the art show this evening, but I still need to talk it out. Lennon will be annoyed. There's no question about it, but I'm a verbal processor, so it has to be done.

I briefly consider calling Cass up instead.

When I pull out my phone, I notice two texts from Finn.

Finn: *What are you wearing?*

Finn: *That was really off brand for me. I'm just practicing for when I leave tomorrow.*

I snort, leaning my elbows on the kitchen island and typing out my response.

Me: *I just assumed you were asking about what to wear for the art show. In that case, a black dress.*

The bubbles pop up as he types his response, and I briefly glance over at Eloise. She officially fell asleep. It's not a good nap, but it's something.

Finn: *And after the show?*

I fight the urge to smile as the room gets warmer–just slightly.

Me: *Probably my retainer.*
Finn: *You're not making this easy.*
Me: *It's more fun when you work for it.*
Finn: *So, you're saying that you want me to–*

I don't finish reading the text message when I hear the front door open. While I am an adult woman in an adult relationship with an adult man, something about being in B and Brian's house makes me feel weird. It's like I'm fifteen all over again.

When I turn to call out down the hallway, I stop, hearing hushed whispers traveling into the kitchen from where they just entered.

B's tone is harsh. "I don't know what the fuck he thinks he's doing cornering us like that."

Brian's deep voice cuts in, low as if he's fighting to keep the conversation private. I decide I'll feel guilty about eavesdropping later. "B, calm down."

"Calm down?" She practically hisses the words, and my heartbeat picks up in my chest. "He can't just show up after all this time–after everything."

Heels click down the hallway, and I turn to greet them when they walk in. Despite the slight frown on Brian's face, there's no sign of the conversation they were just having.

My brow furrows. "Everything okay?"

B blinks. It's like her brain misfires, and she struggles to compute the question.

"Yeah," Brian answers, but there's something in his eyes that tells me that might not be the entire truth.

B shakes her head, gathering herself before her features shift into something more annoyed than anything. She places her bag on the counter, digging around to find her lipstick and reapplying it.

"Just some asshole at the restaurant," she supplies. "No big deal."

If I didn't know better, I'd believe her. B is a damn good liar. But the woman raised me, and I can usually tell when that's not the case.

Still. I let them have their privacy.

A knock sounds at the door, and B looks up, smiling. "Lennon?" she asks. "I'll go get it."

She disappears down the hallway, and Brian offers me a tight-lipped smile before leaving the kitchen.

"You didn't even come to greet me at the door," Lennon complains when she finally enters the room, Aunt B on her tail. "I leave for a week, and you don't pick me up at the airport. You don't come to greet me. Listen," Lennon points a finger in my direction. "I could kill you for this."

"Little ears," B sing-songs as she moves to the fridge to put away whatever leftovers Brian brought in from brunch.

"My sincerest apologies, Lennon." I try to hold back the grin. "How inconvenient for you to have to murder your best friend. I'd send my condolences, but unfortunately. I'll be dead."

She laughs, muttering, "you bitch," before drawing me in for a hug.

"Not to be rude," B starts. "But you two need to get out of here if you're going to be ready for the art show."

When she turns, her eyes are glittering with pride, and something about it does things to my insides. I feel warm and fuzzy, and when our eyes lock for a moment too long, I'm certain B can sense how sappy I'm being.

"I feel most unwelcomed," Lennon complains, but there's no bite to her words.

I give B a rundown on what Eloise ate, the game we played, and how long she'd been sleeping before Lennon and I make our way out the door.

I briefly consider telling her about the conversation I overheard, but decide against it. I'm too nervous about the rapidly approaching art show to think about literally anything else.

That is, until I read the rest of Griffin's text message, and suddenly wish the entire art show was over so he can make good on his promises.

• • • • • • • • • •

"There's our girl!"

I turn around, careful not to spill the champagne in my glass, when I hear the sound of my grandfather's voice.

He draws me in for a hug, smelling of tobacco and pine before he finally releases me.

"I can't believe you're here!" I say, beaming.

Finn places a gentle hand on the small of my back, and I smile up at him before introducing him to my grandfather.

Apparently, B let him know my art would be featured in the exhibit, and he made the trip from New York to be here to see it.

June Peterson's paintings hang on the white walls, decorating the space with images of people so beautifully depicted, you almost feel like you can read their entire story from the canvas.

Lights highlight each of the pieces, and I try to stop my hands from shaking. People have only just been allowed in, and I have yet to go into the room designated for my four large charcoal sketches. The thought of the general public seeing them—judging them—*buying* them—has my stomach twisting into knots and feeling like my intestines will drop right out of my ass.

It would be an unfortunate scene, so with every ounce of wisdom I possess, I briefly consider clenching, but in the tight black dress I'm wearing, it would be too obvious.

"Look at you," Finn says, pressing a kiss to my temple. "I'm so proud of you, Ellie. You deserve this."

My chest expands until I'm certain there's no more room left.

Finn pulls out his phone and checks his messages, pocketing it before giving me an update. "Noah just got here," he says as I see Lennon walk through the door with a man I've never met before.

I'm assuming it's the guy she matched with the other day. She asked if she could bring him to the art show, and while I appreciated her show of sensitivity, I was far more concerned about what the man looked like than if he would be her date or not.

Lennon, of course, refused to show me photos, claiming that she enjoyed surprises.

When I spot the tall blonde at her side, I can't help but smile. For a moment, I thought her lack of information meant he was ugly.

Which he certainly isn't.

"Hey," she says, a soft smile crossing her lips. It's the least abrasive greeting she's ever given, so I try to communicate the words *fake ass bitch* without being incredibly obvious.

I don't think it works, though, because Finn nudges my arm and chuckles.

"Did you want to see June's paintings?" I ask, and Lennon's face falls.

"No, I don't. I literally showed up to see your shit, Ellis." She glances at Finn. "No offense to your mom."

"I don't think she cares."

When Noah walks in behind them from the glass doors, his eyes flick between Lennon and the man she still hasn't introduced us to.

We've had a few get-togethers over the last month, and for some reason, whenever Lennon shows up, Noah has the sudden urge to talk about every date he's ever been on with details nobody wants to know.

So, when his face twists into something I can't recognize, and he ignores both her and her date, it confuses me—just slightly.

Lennon only shrugs.

"Happy for you, Ellie," Noah says, and at the warmth in his words, I can't help but feel some of it, too.

I am happy.

I'm really, really happy.

Twenty-Nine

Griffin

Standing in front of one of my mom's paintings, I allow the lights of the gallery to shine on every brush stroke and mark she created. While guests file in and view my mom's work as art, I just picture painting in the sunroom with one of my dad's T-shirts hanging down to my ankles, and inevitably ruining Storm's artwork by smearing orange all over it.

He used to hate that.

"Griffin." My mom's hand finds my bicep as she sidles up next to me. Wrinkles form at the corners of her eyes, her hair falling into her face–escaping the claw clip she always uses. "Two of Ellie's drawings are gone."

"What?" My heart rate picks up, body suddenly tense at the thought that someone would take one of her–

My mom pats my cheek and laughs. "Settle down, son." Her hazel eyes sparkle in the gallery light–amused at my sudden shift in mood. "People bought them," she finally says.

I must become fucking manic because I'm suddenly soaring. "Have you told her?" I ask, my eyes scanning the room we're in for any sign of Ellie. She's going to lose her shit. I've been listening to her worry about her pieces for weeks, beating herself up and saying she's only part of the show because of my mom. And while that may be true, it doesn't speak on her talent.

Not in the slightest.

My mom smooths down her black turtleneck tucked into whatever shiny cream-colored pants she's wearing. "I thought you'd be the one to let her know." When she looks at me again, she seems so proud. "Anyway," she begins. "Are you ready for your trip tomorrow?"

I nod. "I think so. Ellis is dropping me off at the airport in the morning." I pause, an ache forming in my chest at the thought of leaving her. It's a weird mix of excitement, hope, and sadness–the kind of swirl of emotions that reminds you that you never have to be or feel one thing. "We'll see."

"It'll be good for you to get out and do this." My mom pats my cheek again. "Ellie's a good one, too. She'll support you, and just so you know, we're all very proud of you, Griffin."

I meet her smile with my own before turning back to the painting. "Thanks mom."

My head spins when I hear heels clicking against the light hardwood, seeing Cass determined with her brow furrowed as she makes a straight line to me. "Finn, have you seen Ellis?" she asks.

"No, not in a while. She was off talking to guests."

Cass huffs, folding her arms across her chest, her eyes scanning the room. "Lennon is looking for her. I guess her date left, and now she's on the patio outside the gallery shouting at Noah." For what it's worth, Cass looks stressed. "I think they may kill each other," she mutters.

I chuckle gently sliding past her as my mom disappears into the guests mulling around the room. "I'll find her," I say.

When she's not in the room featuring her drawings, I move toward the patio, but don't see anyone out there aside from a random guest, and Ellie's aunt.

Turning back, I move to the hallway where the bathroom is located, and catch Ellis fiddling with the handle.

I quicken my pace, quickly reaching her and sliding into the single restroom behind her, pulling the door closed and locking it.

She looks stunning–breathtaking. Her hair hangs loose around her shoulders, eyes sparkling with joy. I'm so proud of her, it almost hurts.

I grab her face in my hands and press my mouth to hers. She gasps, slowly melting into the kiss with her hands fisting my suit jacket. "I'm really proud of you, you know," I whisper against her lips before pushing my fingers into her hair and claiming her mouth again.

When I turn her around, pressing her against the bathroom door, she gasps, pulling away. "We can't have sex in this bathroom, Finn."

I move my mouth to her neck. Despite her words, she's still arching her back, leaning into me in a way that drives me wild. I suddenly realize that what she said is actually a great option. It wasn't why I was looking for her, but it seems way better.

"Why not?" I ask, before flicking my tongue out over her flushed skin. Despite her words, she drags me closer.

"Finn," she warns.

I withdraw myself and take a step back. "Fine," I say before pointing a finger at her. "But later, maybe."

She smiles.

"I was actually looking for you to let you know you sold two drawings."

Ellis leaps into my arms, and I stumble back, catching her around the waist. Her laugh vibrates against my chest. "Oh my God," she says. When she breaks away, she presses her hands to my shoulders. "You're serious?"

"Yes, and your ass looks great in that dress. I wanted to tell you that, too."

She doesn't seem to notice. It's like she's flying above the clouds—too busy to pay my desires any mind. "I sold two drawings!" she echoes.

"Yes, and did you catch the part about your ass?"

She swats at me before squealing. "Yes, I heard you, but I'm too excited." She glances at the toilet in the corner. "Okay, I really have to go. Get out of here before someone thinks we're having sex."

I laugh, moving toward the door to sneak out, but I pause when I hear her voice again.

"Oh!" she starts. "Go find Lennon. Cass told me she was yelling at Noah on the patio."

I turn back, the smile still stuck to my face. "I heard about that."

When she practically pushes me out, I make my way into the hallway, finding a guest standing and waiting for the bathroom.

I smooth down my tie and offer them a friendly expression. "Someone's still in there, sorry."

The look of horror on the woman's face is enough to provide comedic relief for days.

I move through the rooms of the gallery, finding the French doors at the back toward the patio. Muffled sounds leak through, and I'm left staring at the random guest I saw earlier, a tall man with a gruff beard and a suit that doesn't quite fit.

Ellie's aunt is out there too, and she looks pissed. Brian is nowhere to be found.

When I open the doors, the muffled sounds turn to all out shouting, and I'm left wondering if Cass was right about who was on the patio fighting.

"You still can't just show up here!" B shouts. She's rounding on the man, and for what it's worth, I'd be afraid of her, too.

He stumbles back, holding his hands up in defense. "I just wanted to meet her," he says. "I saw her name for the art show and thought—"

B doesn't let him finish. "You thought *wrong*, Adam." She huffs out a breath, and I'm fairly certain she's about to turn into a dragon. I can feel the heat from here. "You've done some really shitty things, including leaving her mother, but this far outweighs all of that. Let Ellis enjoy her time tonight."

At the sound of her voice, I insert myself into the conversation, clearing my throat and wondering if I'm cut out to be art show security. It's a rapid career change, but when I see that I'm taller than the man, I think I may have a chance. "What's going on?" I ask, trying to deescalate the situation.

"Finn," B says, as if she just realized I'd come out to the patio. The warm spring air has cooled with the late hour, and I'm suddenly thankful for the full suit.

"Who are you?" I ask, turning to the man standing and looking worse for the wear.

"Adam, don't," B warns.

Adam's jaw clenches when he looks at her, and he straightens. Something in his eyes looks predatory–determined. "You know Ellis Smalley?"

My brow furrows. "She's my girlfriend. Why?"

I don't miss B's muttered *fuck*, and the click of the French doors behind me before his answer steals the breath from my lungs.

"I'm her father."

There's a harsh intake of breath behind me, and when I turn, I see Ellis with a confused look on her face. It's a look that reminds me she's never met the man before.

"B?" she questions, her voice sounding weak. "Who is this?"

Thirty

Ellis

I never put cliff diving on the bucket list I gave to Finn back in December, but by the sheer lack of oxygen in my lungs, I'm starting to think the universe took some liberties.

"B?" I question, though my voice sounds shaky. "Who is this?"

It's stupid, because I just heard the man announce that he was my father, but I need some kind of confirmation.

"Ellis," B's voice sounds distant. "This is Adam. He dated your mom for a time." I can tell by her expression alone that what he said was the truth. "He's your biological father."

I nod. I will not cry out on this patio–not here. The man before me is a stranger, standing in front of me in an ill-fitted suit–looking like he just rolled out of bed before showing up at an art show. "I think," I start, feeling Finn slide in next to me, his strong arm tucking me closer to him. I'm thankful for it. "I think that maybe this isn't a great time to do this," I finally say, thankful that my voice isn't wavering as much as before.

I haven't had a chance to process or think. The first thing that hits me is the feeling of stupidity. I should have guessed more was going on when I heard B and Brian arguing earlier today. Whatever high I had from selling my art has vanished. I'm falling, and I don't really know how to slow down.

On one hand, I'm pissed. On the other hand–

I don't really know.

"I think maybe it would be best if you leave," Finn says, his grip tightening on my shoulder as I cling to him.

"We can talk about this tomorrow?" I look at B questioningly. "Give him my number?"

"You're sure?" she asks, and I nod.

I turn to Finn, seeing the warmth in his gaze and it settles some of my swirling emotions. "Am I allowed to go home?" I whisper.

"You're allowed to do whatever you want, Ellis."

We leave the patio as Brian rushes through the door.

• • • • ● ● ● • • •

"You want to talk about it?"

Streetlights pass outside the Jeep windows, lighting the car before plunging it back into darkness. It seems like a good metaphor for my emotions, to be honest.

I've spent a lot of time feeling like I was thrown into B's life in a way that nobody truly wanted, and while I don't question her love for me, I *am* reminded of the things Lennon and Griffin said back in December. I do a lot to shoulder the burden of my own existence when I don't need to.

"It could be a good thing," I say, but my voice is quiet.

"Okay," Finn says, his hands firmly fixed to the steering wheel. His eyes stay glued to the road. "Okay, good. Keep going."

"B never talked about him much. My mom didn't either. It might be good to hear him out." Something wraps around my heart and squeezes. It feels sort of like the truth, so I let it out. "I've already had one parent taken from me. I guess I'm shocked, but I also have hope."

Finn lets out a heavy breath, one that tells me he'd been holding it in for a while. "That makes me feel a little better." There's a pause as the Jeep goes dark again.

"It could be terrible too," I admit. "There's a reason he was never around, and there's a reason nobody cared to talk about it."

Finn's eyes slide to me, and I notice the way he flexes his fingers at the wheel. "I can tell Ryland I can't do the show."

"What?" I ask, my voice loud as I sit up. "No! Griffin, you can't do that."

"I can," he says. "It's fine, Ellie. Other opportunities will come. I just don't feel right about leaving you for two weeks after this."

"No." The word is a firm order. "I'm fully capable of handling this on my own."

"You handle a lot on your own."

My brow furrows. "No, I don't. Lennon and Cass will be here, and you'll still have a cell phone. It's not like you're going off to war."

"I might not be able to respond during the shows." When I look at his shoulders, I can see tension there. "Or if we don't have service wherever we're driving." He slows the car as we pull in front of my house, putting it in park before turning toward me.

His smile is nowhere to be found, and the realization cuts sharp like a blade.

"No," I say again, more confident. "You're going to go on this tour, Finn. You're going to go, and you're going to enjoy yourself. I will be here when you get back."

I don't let him respond. I pull at the handle, and flee the vehicle. If he gets too soft, I may just melt into him–like a damn popsicle. I refuse to be the reason he stays in Ohio forever without ever exploring the opportunities out on the road. I refuse to make him sacrifice that for me.

I fumble with the keys, quickly inserting them into the lock when he comes up behind me.

When we're both in the house, he takes my face firmly in his hands, crashing his lips into mine, and I stumble back. His mouth demands attention, his tongue tracing the seam of my lips until I let him in.

It doesn't take much.

It never has.

Finn convinced me he was trustworthy in a coffee shop with roughly thirty minutes of questioning.

When he pulls away, his chest is rising and falling at a rapid pace, as if he placed all of his emotions into the kiss—as if he needed it, too.

"Okay," he finally agrees, resting his forehead against mine. "But you *will* call me if you need me, Ellie."

I nod. "I will."

"And if I don't have service on the road, I'll pen you a letter or something."

I laugh, wrapping my arms around his waist and pulling him in. Finn grips the back of my head, his thumb stroking over my hair.

"I'm in love with you, Ellie."

I blink, not sure if I heard him right.

"I'm so fucking in love with you. I think I knew it the moment I met you."

My fingers fist the back of his shirt, clinging on for dear life. "I'm in love with you, too."

Thirty-One

Griffin

Night stretches on outside of the bedroom windows as I pull Ellie closer to my chest.

I considered staying at least three more times. Especially when she talked about meeting her dad for dinner in a few days. I want to be here so fucking bad, but she's right.

It would be so easy to let fear guide me—to build that wall around my heart—the one that keeps me in place. I've spent a lot of time craving stability. So much time that I've forgotten how to go after the things I want.

Even so, leaving her eats away at something deep inside of me.

When she shifts even closer, I plant a kiss on her shoulder, memorizing the feel of her tucked close–thinking of how much I'm going to miss her.

My arm wraps around her, thumb tucking beneath the fabric of her shirt, drawing slow circles against her stomach.

She places her hand over mine, her touch warm. When she presses back into me, everything tightens. My hand stops moving, and I gently press my hips forward, dragging a soft sound from her lips.

"Ellie," I whisper, and her hand tightens over mine, slowly dragging it down her stomach, dipping beneath the waistband of her sleep shorts.

I groan, pressing my hips forward again as she meets the motion with her own.

"Remember what you said in the bathroom?" Her voice is soft like the skin beneath my fingertips.

"I thought maybe we'd press pause on that." But *fuck*. I don't want to.

Ellis flips over, removing my hand from her and giving me a hard look. "Absolutely not, Griffin. You're leaving for two weeks."

I smile, bringing my palm up to up her cheek as I kiss her. "It's Finn," I say against her lips.

"Finn." she corrects.

I carefully pull at the hem of her shirt, dragging it over her head when she leans up to help me. My own shirt is the next to go, followed by pants and underwear until we're both stripped down and tangled together.

"I'm going to miss you," she whispers, and it pulls at something in my chest.

I reach over to the nightstand, rolling on the condom before lining myself up with her. "I know," I say, brushing a soft kiss to the corner of her mouth. "I'm going to miss you, too."

This time, something shifts. It's as if our own words linger in the air, hanging like stars above us—shining light on everything in the room.

It's a truth that sounds louder than the worries of the coming weeks.

I'm in love with her.

• • • • • • • • •

Ellis stares at her phone as I drive through the short-term parking garage at the airport, unable to stop glancing over.

"What is it?" I ask.

Her brow furrows as she types a reply to whatever text she just got.

"Ellie?"

"Shush," she scolds. "I can't focus on you and type this at the same time."

I huff a laugh, pulling into a parking lot near the entrance and shutting off the car.

When she's done, she looks up at me. "B wants to meet before I have dinner with Adam. I'm a little nervous, but I don't want to worry you."

I reach across the console and thread my fingers through hers. "I'm not worried," I say, a wide smile breaking across my face.

"Liar," she says, her lips pulling up at one corner.

I lean in, tightening my grip on her hand. "Prove it," I say, before planting a quick kiss to her mouth.

When we get out of the car, we walk toward the baggage check-in, and I'm thankful that the airport has switched over to kiosks instead of forcing everyone to talk to employees up front. For one, it goes way faster. For two, this flight is fucking early.

We walk hand in hand to the line for TSA, and I draw her to me, trying to memorize the feel of her. "It's only two weeks," I say.

She chuckles. "Yes, exactly. I'm not sure why you're acting like you're going off to war."

"It could turn into more weeks if I do a decent enough job."

Ellie pulls away, her brown eyes flicking between mine. There's a question buried in my words, one that I already know the answer to. I still need to hear it. "And that will be a *good* thing, Finn." She presses a palm to my cheek and strokes the pad of her thumb across my jaw. "I'm going to be alright."

I kiss her again before dragging my suitcase behind me to get in line.

She waits until I'm through to the other side before turning, and I can't help but feel like I've left part of myself here—back in Ohio.

Thirty-Two

Ellis

I've never been more thankful for my boring job that I'm not passionate about. As I stare at the computer screen, my leg involuntarily bounces beneath the desk. I don't know why I agreed to meet with Adam today, and I don't know what B is going to say about it when I stop there before the dinner.

My body is a giant pile of nerves, and staring at my monitor, I find that working suddenly feels like procrastination.

And I'm a whore for procrastination.

A chair creaks on the other side of the divider and I see Rupert's head pop into view. "How are you doing there, Ellie?" he asks.

My leg stops bouncing. "Hmm?" I ask, before swiveling to face him.

"Well," he begins. "For one, I can feel you fidgeting from over here. You're shaking the entire floor." He rolls his chair around the bend, now fully in my cubicle. "For two, you've said nothing all day, and you didn't even wrinkle your nose when I came back from lunch." A small smile pulls at his mouth, highlighting the deep wrinkles there. "I ate tuna, so I know how that was supposed to go."

I make a strange noise. It's something like laughter mixed with a heavy dose of embarrassment and shame. I'm not even sure I could repeat something like that.

"So," Rupert says, resting his elbows on his knees and clasping his hands in front of him. He wrings them out. "Tell me what's on your mind. You thinking about quitting after that art show of yours? I know you were excited."

I lean back in my chair. "Actually, no. My artwork did well, though. That was exciting! I think maybe I can do both." I shrug. "It's not so bad here."

His brow furrows. "That boyfriend didn't–"

I cut him off. "Finn and I are great. He's finally got an opportunity to tour with a band he loves. He'll be back in about a little over a week."

Rupert sits up, crossing his arms over his chest in a way that straightens some of the wrinkles in his checkered button-down shirt. "Okay, so what is it then?"

I debate telling him. I debate it for a whole twelve seconds before I give in. It might be nice to talk to someone outside of the situation. "My dad showed up at the art show."

"Your dad?"

"I've never met him before. He never stuck around, and then he was just there. Arguing with my aunt on the patio."

Rupert's brows pinch together. "And what was he there for?"

I shrug, trying to squelch the little bubble of hope in my chest. What nobody tells you about losing someone is that a hole forms in you. Sometimes you don't notice it, and it's a little more like Swiss cheese. It stops feeling *wrong* and feels more like *it just is*. But when something happens to remind you it's there, that's when the ache starts up again.

I don't want to hope that meeting my dad will ease the ache. Not with his history.

But the hope is still there.

"I guess he wants to meet me." I shake my head. "But I don't know. B, my aunt, was pretty pissed off seeing him there. He's done a lot of really shitty things in the past."

Rupert slides forward and motions for my hand. For whatever reason, I let him take it. He's sitting in front of me, eyes shining with wisdom—gentle and warm.

"Listen, Ellie," he begins, and I hold my breath. It feels like he's about to say something important. "I've picked up on pieces of your life over the years you've worked here. I've watched you grow as an employee. As a person. I even suffered in the dungeon with you. It was unreasonable."

I laugh, biting back the tears threatening to leak out of my eyes. "It was really terrible down there."

Rupert smiles. "Sometimes men come around. Sometimes they find whatever it was they were looking for in the strangest of places. They get the help they need. Maybe they start therapy, or maybe it's an accident that wakes them up." He presses his lips together, patting the top of my hand with his other before continuing. "Sometimes men come around and see what they've been missing, and they're there to stay."

I can hear the word before he says it. "But?" I add.

"But, sometimes they don't." I blink, that hole in my chest aching. "Whatever happens when or if you decide to meet this man, you remember a couple of things. You do not owe him for existing. You are not a burden that your aunt had to carry for your mother." A tear spills down my cheek, blazing a trail before I wipe it away with my free hand. "And most importantly, you can always–*always*–walk away. You want to let this man into your life, then you go right ahead and do it. But if you don't, there's no sense in feeling guilty. He made a choice all those years ago, and we are all responsible for our own choices."

Rupert pats my hand another time, winks at me, and rolls his chair back around until I'm left sitting in my cubicle with tear stains on my nice work shirt.

I grab my phone off the desk and text Finn.

Me: *I miss you.*

His response is almost immediate.

Finn: *I love you.*

• • • • • • • • •

B's porch light is on when I pull into the driveway. I don't even make it out of the car before she comes out, a large cardigan wrapped around her, and her eyes puffy and pink.

Has she been crying?

I step out of the car. "Hey," I say.

B wraps her arms around me, holding me in a tight hug. I melt into her, allowing the familiar scent of oranges and spice to soothe my nerves.

"I love you, you know that?" Her voice is muffled from where her face presses into my hair. "I love you so fucking much, Ellie. And I'm so sorry. I know you don't understand why we never talked about him, but that man was shit. Absolute shit."

I tighten my grip on her. It's been a long time since I've seen B break apart. She's always been so strong.

B pulls away, wiping her face before placing her hands on my shoulders. "I'm not trying to keep you here, Ellie. You're a grown woman, and a damn good one at that. I don't know how it happened, but you became everything I could have ever hoped for."

I nod, not really knowing what to say.

"I believe in second chances, so I'm not going to tell you anything to sway you one direction or the other, but just know that no matter what happens, we love you."

She places a kiss on my cheek and walks away, leaving me staring after her in the driveway.

• • • ● • ● • ● • • •

My knee is shaking again when the waiter comes around a third time to ask if I'm ready to order. I reassure him I'm waiting on someone, but he doesn't seem to believe me.

Looking toward the door, I notice Adam walk in. Between his mussed hair, the untrimmed beard, and the harsh look on his face, I can't see anything in him that reminds me of myself.

But when Adam sits across from me at the table, his brown eyes boring into my own, I finally see it.

"Hey, kid."

My fingers clasp around the glass of water, drawing in a long sip. It's already awkward. "Hi," I say.

Adam picks up the menu, and I watch him scan the entrees. Since I've been waiting on him, I already know what I'll be ordering.

The waiter comes around and we place our orders.

"So, you came to the art show because—" I let my words trail off at the end, waiting for Adam to fill in the blanks.

"Thought it was about time I met my daughter," he says, offering a half smile. The expression is gone before it even appears. Adam picks up a piece of bread from the center of the table and stuffs it in his mouth. "Heard your mom died. Saw your name for that art show, and figured it was about time."

I wince, taking another sip of water to soothe the burning in my throat. "My mom died when I was thirteen," I say. "How far do you live if you saw my name advertised for the show?"

Adam presses his elbow to the table, making a show of thinking about my question. "Oh, you know." He taps his fingers on the white tablecloth. "Two hours or so."

An uncomfortable feeling stirs in my gut, something nagging–dark. "You're just now wanting to meet me?" I ask. "And you live that close?"

He offers another one of those half done smiles, and my stomach churns. "First time for everything."

I nod and silence stretches across the table as we wait.

When our food comes, I'm thankful for something to do. Each bite feels like lead as my mind mulls over the entire interaction. He spent all this time living so close and never thought about stopping by until now?

"So," he starts as he stabs his steak with a fork. "Probably pretty rough to lose your mom like that. She was something."

My stomach twists, warning bells ringing loudly in my head. "Yeah," I say. "She really was."

He hums, taking a bite of steak and then washing it down with the beer he ordered. "You get a good chunk of change when that happened?"

Everything inside of me burns hot. My chest feels like it's going to bubble over, pouring my rage all over the dinner I can't stomach. "Excuse me?" I ask.

Brown eyes meet mine, but this time when I look, I don't see anything of myself reflected back. I see someone hollow.

"I mean, she had cancer, right? I got contacted toward the end or whatever. She knew for a while." He wipes his mouth with his napkin. "If she knew she was going to die, she probably had a pretty good life insurance policy."

"You were contacted?" My lungs expand and deflate too rapidly, my ears drowning out the noise of the restaurant around me. I reach for my bag beneath my chair, gripping it like it will save me from punching this man in the face.

"I mean, yeah," he says. "I knew about you. But I was tied up at the time. I was dating this woman, and thought we'd get married. It wasn't exactly the right time for a kid, you know?"

My teeth grind together. Memories of B walking across a stage at her college graduation, memories of the funeral, my grandfather trying his best to help—it all flashes through my mind like a movie. "I can imagine," I say.

The waiter comes around asking if we need anything, and I'm pretty sure I'm seconds away from combusting.

"The check," I say, and Adam smiles—a feral expression that sends me close to tipping over the edge. As if I could get any closer.

"So, she did leave you with a chunk of change, kid."

Without another word, I stand up, throwing my bag over my shoulder and walking to the counter. After making up some fake explanation for why I need to pay immediately, I charge my unfinished meal and pay for my father's, too.

And when I get to the parking lot–alone–I let the tears spill out of me.

Thirty-Three

Griffin

When I get backstage after the show, I finally plug my phone in, resting my head against the wall behind the hard ass chair I fell into.

The door to the room creeks open, and Ryland shows up with the four other band members following behind him.

He runs a hand through his sweaty hair, and grabs a water from the fridge, throwing himself onto the couch where he places his feet on the coffee table. "So," he says, glancing in my direction. "How are you liking the road, Griffin?" There's a smile plastered on his face.

It's the second show I've played since joining the guys on tour, and I'd be lying to say I don't enjoy it. For starters, I'm not mixing anything I don't like. The live shows are thrilling, the tech side is something I'm good at. I briefly recall mixing a song that sucked back in December. It was the song that had me feeling like I'd wasted my entire childhood dreaming of doing something with music.

This band—this tour—makes me feel like it was all worth it.

"I fucking love it," I say, picking up my phone. The thing must have been really dead, considering the red battery is still popping up on the screen.

"That's good." Ryland takes another swig of water. "Want to make this something a little more permanent?"

My heart is beating faster in my chest, the excitement making some of my exhaustion disappear. "That would be awesome, man." I run a hand down my face, barely able to keep up. "I mean, I'd have to talk about it with Ellie when I get back, but I would definitely consider something like that."

"Ah, the girl," he says. "She has to approve, for sure. My wife would plot my murder if she found out my guys were making decisions without approval." He chuckles, and I press the lock button on my phone again, watching the screen light up.

A number of missed calls come through, all from Ellie, and my heart sinks.

Before I click on her number, I read the text message.

Ellie: *I think he only wanted money.*

"Fuck," I mutter.

I grab the portable charger out of my bag, plug my phone in and excuse myself. Finding a quiet place in the venue where I actually have service.

The phone rings longer than expected, and when she picks up, I can hear it in her voice.

She's been crying.

"What happened?" I ask. "I'll fly home right now. What the fuck happened, Ellie?"

Regret slices through me as I question my selfishness. I shouldn't have left her. I should have stayed behind–been there when she needed me. I should have–

"Don't," she says, and though her voice shakes, she sounds anything but weak. "I just want to talk for a minute. Do you have time?"

There's no question.

"Of course I have time."

Thirty-Four

Ellis

When I was fourteen, B put me into therapy.

I don't like talking about it. At the time, I'd been embarrassed and frustrated–ashamed even.

To be perfectly honest, I was just a kid. B was just a kid, too. Our days were riddled with hopeless fumbling and trying to make sense of the new normal while grieving the loss of my mother–her sister.

It had been a complete year since the death of my mom. I'd been okay for a while after she died. It was like the adrenaline rush of tragedy numbed my emotions and held me together when I needed it most. Shock can sometimes feel like that.

Days went by with her being sick, but I clung to the hope of it all the entire time without even realizing what I was doing, and at the end of that first year with her gone, the sorrow hit me like an oncoming train.

I'd been old enough to see the toll my mother's death had taken on my aunt. At the start of my freshman year of high school, I realized just how much *struggle* was happening, and I didn't want to add to it. So, when B sat me down at our dinky kitchen table, the one with coffee rings that seemed engraved into the wood like permanent scars, I couldn't help but feel like I was making her life harder.

B didn't need harder.

A lot of time was spent keeping B from that difficulty. Maybe that's the real reason I never asked about my dad. *No*. Adam. It took that man all of two seconds to show his real colors. I suppose he wasn't worth asking about to begin with.

As I watch the ceiling fan spin above my bed, I can't help but wonder if I'm doing the same thing to Griffin when it comes to my dad. Feelings and memories haunt me, and they're relentless. It's like the pain of those memories grew roots. Memories are like weeds in the garden, the same ones starting to crop up in front of my house. I can pull the plant out, but for some reason I can never be rid of the thing–not truly. It's like every season, I have to keep digging–fixing up the plot of earth I desperately wanted to be beautiful.

My memories of my mom are like that. The therapy helped. The years have helped, but every once in a while, something triggers it all to start again.

My father planted weeds in the garden.

I glance at the clock beside my bed, the glowing blue numbers telling me it's way too late for me to still be awake considering it's a work night. Four AM is the hour for sadness, I suppose. The feelings have already taken shape–so I might as well feel them while I'm here. I can be fine tomorrow.

Dragging myself out of bed, I give up on sleep entirely as I pad to the closet and flick the light on. With brightness stinging my eyes, I rummage around until I find the old shoe box shoved toward the back. There's a thread tied around my heart that tugs me to its contents–an invisible thread, but a thread all the same.

Simon winds between my legs as I shuffle back to the bed, trying to dodge him. When I flick on the dim lamp seated on top of the nightstand, I crawl to the center of the bed, and Simon quickly hops up to join me.

I run my finger across the lid, and images start to take shape in my mind.

"It will be good for you, Ellis."

B's voice echoes like a faint whisper. I can still see her sitting across from me, concern carving a line between her brows and dark circles painting the blue color beneath her eyes.

A tear trails down my cheek, and I wipe it away. Chiding myself for my weakness.

Somewhere between the art show and dinner, I had started to hope–just like I did with mom when she was in the hospital. I hadn't even realized I'd done it. At least, not to this extent.

"You're wandering around like a ghost. You've shut down, and my therapist told me I need to tell you it's okay because it is. It's a normal part of grief, but I'm worried. I wasn't supposed to say that part. At least I don't think. Maybe I just wasn't supposed to say it like that."

My stomach feels like lead as the whisper of a memory grows louder.

"I don't know what I'm doing, Ellie." She sounds desperate. "I want you to see the therapist," B finishes as shame colors my cheeks. It isn't supposed to be like this. I wasn't supposed to make her life hard. It was supposed to be me and mom. It was supposed to be us now–forever.

B was supposed to be the fun aunt I got to visit once a week. She was never supposed to look this defeated.

"I'm sorry," the words are out before I can reel them back in, and her shoulders tense.

"Christ." The word comes out like a curse–dirty. It's as if the man who inspired it hadn't lived up to his name–like he let us down.

I can see how it would happen though–I'm letting B down.

"Don't be upset," I whisper.

"I'm not upset, Ellis!"

I flinch. I've never heard her yell before, and it sounds an awful lot like I might be the reason she's losing her grip on her emotions.

Don't cry. I cannot cry. It will only make things worse.

"I'll go," I say. "To therapy, I mean."

Trailing my finger over one of the coffee rings on the table, I think about all the scars slashed across our hearts. The least I can do is keep myself from adding any more.

I stand up. If I cry in front of B, then it will really be my fault. Whatever she needs. I'll be or do whatever she needs. Mom would have wanted it that way.

The lid to the shoebox opens with a gentle flick of my thumb, and there she is.

Bright like sunshine, my mother is smiling beneath a canopy of trees. I can remember taking the photo when I was seven on an old film camera. When we got it developed , I saw how happy it made my mom to see herself the way I saw her. Nobody took pictures of her. I didn't have a dad like the other kids, and so I promised myself I would keep taking pictures.

I run my finger along the photo before gently removing it to reveal another. In this one, I'm younger–four years old in my grandmother's kitchen with flour on my face. My mom's sleeves are rolled up as she presses her palm firmly into the dough on the counter. She'd always loved making bread, and I loved that I got to play with the extra. It made me feel special.

There's another photo and another. I'm crying in earnest, letting the night wash over me as I continue my journey through the forbidden.

There's a fine line between allowing yourself to feel, and allowing your feelings to swallow you whole–taking those you love right down with them, but if I keep this all to myself, then maybe I will be the only one in the pit.

After talking to Griffin, I felt better, but I could still hear the worry in his tone. It was in the way he said he'd fly home. He'd give up his dreams for me when they were barely just beginning.

I already had someone give up their dream for me—or at least, postpone it.

I pick up another picture. Me and mom dancing in the living room.

A baby photo where B is holding me and my mom is smiling at her.

There's a picture of my grandfather teaching me how to shoot a bow. Mom smiling. Mom cooking. Mom looking thinner. Mom's smile turning sadder.

My tears drip into the box, filling it as I empty all the emotions returning from so long ago. Maybe they will never leave.

When the sea of photos surrounds me, and I get to the last one at the bottom of the box, my heart clenches. It's a picture of my mom in the hospital—a shadow of who she was before. I can barely recognize myself in the photo—like sadness morphed me into someone I couldn't possibly know.

Simon purrs at the end of the bed, curled in a ball and undisturbed by the disaster I've created. When my phone buzzes, his eyes peek open.

Griffin's name pops up and read the worried text. I can't help but feel ridiculous for wallowing in my sorrow. I've let a stranger cause me to become completely unglued.

So, my dad is an asshole. I knew that from the beginning. The problem is, when he showed up, I started *wanting*. I hadn't realized how much I wanted until that dangerous hope bloomed in my chest. Then I realized what was happening at that damn restaurant and the weeds killed whatever goodness had become of the meeting.

I text Griffin back, letting him know that I'm fine. I tell him our talk really helped, which is the truth, and that I have work today.

I *will* be fine. When the morning comes, I'll put my head down and keep going.

He texts back almost immediately, and it reminds me of how worried he is. If he saw me now–heard my voice–he'd come home. I know how important this step was to him, and I cannot be the thing that holds him back.

I decide not to answer.

Dragging myself off the bed, I leave the photos scattered around. The whole house feels cold and dark when I make my way to the bathroom, but the brush of fur at my ankles provides a small relief. Simon's warm body reminds me of the warmth of Finn's chest, and the way his smile cracks across his face–brightening everything about him.

Finn is happy.

I want to hold that happy, keep my hands steady as I protect it with my life. My tears won't stain the precious thing we've built. I won't let them.

<h1 style="text-align:center">Thirty-Five</h1>

Griffin

She didn't answer.

I couldn't stop staring at my phone as the tour bus plowed down the open highway, racing just as fast as my heart.

Worry wrapped around me from one state to the next until I found myself consumed by it and questioning all of my choices to leave when I did. I know Ellis would have never let me stay–she would have felt guilty, but it would have been worth it if she needed me.

Ryland plucks at a guitar from a stool, his voice winding through the fancy equipment on stage, floating over floors that will no doubt be sticky by the night's end.

I try to distract myself by listening and thinking about work, but Ryland isn't using any of the equipment. He's just doing something he loves, which is exactly how I've felt since joining them on this tour. For the first time in my life, I've allowed myself to leave my family—my home. I'm chasing after something new, but at the same time, my home had just gotten bigger. The circle of people I care about—people I could lose—got bigger.

Leaning back in my chair, I pull the hood of my sweatshirt up and put my arms behind my head. Ryland is just fucking around as he plays "The Girl" by City and Colour from the stage. The reality of touring is that we spend a lot of time fucking around with the instruments.

It means I have a lot of time to think about Ellis.

I close my eyes, letting the words take shape in my mind, painting a picture of her, her hair tucked behind her ear as she scratches charcoal across paper. An image of her climbing a chain linked fence in the middle of December flashes through my mind. She'd been glowing that night.

So much of that time with Ellis had been spent being something different than what I'd been since my brother died. I stopped being so afraid and started letting go.

A far more harrowing picture of her replaces the images of how happy she was. It's Ellis alone, the corners of her pink lips tilted downward, eyes glistening with tears she refuses to let anyone see.

The guitar stops, but I hardly notice.

When my brother died, I held on to everyone and everything–afraid they'd all slip away without warning. Something about the text–the *I'm fine* feels just like that. Slipping away.

I'm haunted by the loss all over again. The feeling of hunkering down and clinging to the familiar.

"You good, man?"

No.

I open my eyes and iron out the crease that formed between my brows, my hands still casually placed on the back of my head. "For tonight?" I say. "Yeah. All is good."

Ryland grunts as he moves even closer with the guitar still clutched in his tattooed hand. "Not the show. Something else." A metal chair screeches as he drags it across the floor, sitting himself far enough that I don't feel crowded, but close enough that I know we are about to have a conversation–one I'd rather be having with Noah if he'd answer his phone.

"I'm good," I assure. It's my last ditch effort at hiding the weight on my chest, making it hard to breathe.

"Nah," he says casually, setting the guitar on the floor. "What's up?"

I run my hand down my face, sighing as I give into whatever this strange intervention is about to be. Ryland and I are friends–I think. Being crowded on a tour bus, haunted by the worst gas station food shits will do that. Those damn ghosts lurk around every corner–just like the memories threatening to drag me under.

I'm so damn tempted to get on a flight and just *leave*.

"What do you do when shit happens at home?" I ask. "With your wife and kids, I mean?" It's a real question. I don't know how anyone can do this–how they can hold on to their relationships while being gone.

Ryland chuckles, placing his elbows on his knees as he clasps his hands together. "I'd be lying to you if I said it was easy. My family is my number one regardless of what I choose to do with my career." He taps a thumb on the back of his other hand. "We have a good support system. I'm not the only one who can take care of my wife, and it would be selfish to think I was. She'd say she can take care of herself, I guess." A smile splits his face. "She'd say it even when the car breaks down, but deep down we both know her dad saves her ass on that one every time."

I nod, acknowledging what he's saying, my mind still swirling with worry.

"Your girl okay?" he asks, breaking the silence.

"Not entirely." Looking up at the lights hanging from the ceiling, the pent up stress leaves me in a whoosh. I swear that one fucking breath says more than I ever could.

"Call in back up," Ryland says as if it's simple. "If you want it bad enough, you can take care of your own from anywhere for a time–as long as at the end of the day–or tour, rather–you come back home."

Ryland doesn't say anything more. He just gets up and strides away, headed toward the trashy dressing room this venue put us in.

I pull my phone out of my pocket, my stomach churning at the sight of Ellis's last texts. She's been quiet for days. It's like I can feel her disappearing, and I'm afraid that when I wake up–she will be gone.

There are two kinds of death in this world. There's the physical one that I experienced with my brother–the same death she experienced with her mom. But there's an emotional death, too. And both kinds of death take people away.

I don't want her to be alone or disappear.

Fighting my fear, I click on a name I never touch. When Lennon picks up, I stumble over my words, but it doesn't matter.

Ryland is right. It's selfish to think I'm the only one who can take care of my girl. While I'm chasing my dreams, she didn't once complain even though her world started crumbling around her. Even if I'm not there, Ellis has a whole host of people who love her. She'd never forgive herself if I came home, but that doesn't mean I don't want to be there for her.

I *will* be there for her.

I'm not letting her slip away from me.

I'm not losing anyone.

Not if I can help it.

Thirty-Six

Ellis

The clock hanging above the television in my living room ticks, time moving forward despite my ability to move with it.

Sometime after dinner, the phone call with Griffin, the night I spent crying, I dried up my tears and turned on autopilot. I go to work. I come home. I make food—mostly frozen pizza or leftover takeout. I turn the television off, and then I listen to the clock for a few minutes before going to bed.

My saving grace was watching Eloise yesterday. For the entire evening, my mind was void of the memory of Adam's comments and the hole in my chest that somehow started feeling like a fucking crater.

Eloise could sense it, placing her little hands on my face and telling me I looked sad. She insisted that being scared was far better than sad and proceeded to drag me into the living room to play scary coffee shop again. This time, I didn't tire of the game.

When B got home, I spilled my guts to her. She already knew what happened, but somehow, every ounce of everything I ever felt came out in those conversations.

I told her I felt like a burden. I told her I was afraid to pursue anything unstable, but when I really thought about it, my job was alright.

The crater in my chest filled in a bit when she hugged me, and that was something.

I am alright, though.

Standing from my spot on the couch, I move toward the kitchen, shuffling through the mail on my table, and remembering that I need to pay my electric bill. I cannot be late. The damn electric company doesn't care if you're in a coma, they will get their money.

Simon brushes against my leg, and I look down before scratching him behind the ears. "You miss him, don't you?" I ask, and he seems to understand. Or maybe I'm just going crazy. "I do, too."

A knock sounds at the door, and my brow furrows as Simon scurries away.

I briefly consider grabbing the longest book I own for defense before I decide against it.

Lennon and Cass stand in the dim porch light. Cass holds up a clear plastic bag with what looks to be no less than three pints of ice cream.

"Surprise!" she says.

Lennon huffs a breath. "I told her I wouldn't say that. It was dumb, but we are here with ice cream. Let us invade your space."

I laugh, grinning as they both step into my apartment. Thank God I haven't lost the motivation to clean. I'm not that depressed.

"Why are you guys here?" I ask, quickly flicking on an extra lamp as Lennon helps herself to all the silverware my kitchen holds. The noise rattles through the house, and I start to question if she's okay.

"Finn called us. He gets back in a few days, and thought we should check in again." Cass's blue eyes look worried, and I suddenly realize why Finn invited them over.

"He told you I cried on the phone, didn't he?"

Cass cringes. "Well," she says, dragging the word out like she doesn't want to admit to espionage or whatever this qualifies as.

When Lennon appears again with three spoons, she throws herself on the couch and flicks the television on. "Of course he told us that," she says. "And it was uncomfortable, but he loves you, so we complied."

"For the record." Cass sets the ice cream down on the coffee table. "I was not uncomfortable at all."

We crowd onto the couch, settling on an episode of *New Girl* before digging into the pints of ice cream they bought. Whatever flavor Lennon purchased is far better than any popsicle I've ever had.

Between the show, the pajamas, Finn's inappropriate texts, and the ice cream, some of the numbness of the last week starts to fade.

When the clock hits one in the morning, I become suddenly aware of every birthday I've ever had.

"It's late," I announce.

Cass is practically snoring on the couch, and Lennon is shoveling handfuls of popcorn into her mouth as she laughs at the screen. "We're staying here," she says.

I smile, looking down at my hands in my lap. "Okay," I say, my voice low.

My phone vibrates on the coffee table, and I pick it up. Opening the screen to the newest texts from Finn.

Finn: *I hope they brought you good ice cream flavors. Lennon said you liked some lavender one. I told her it sounded weird, and she proceeded to lecture me about how she's known you longer.*

I snort, drawing Lennon's attention away from the bowl of popcorn on her lap.

Finn: *I also can't wait to see you. You know, I thought we could–*

"Oh, disgusting!"

I quickly lock my phone, looking at Lennon's mortified expression. I can't help the way my cheeks flame, knowing she read that last message. I don't dare respond–not with her present.

"You're the one who looked," I say.

Lennon stands up, grabbing our empty cartons of ice cream before fleeing to the kitchen. "I wasn't aware Griffin could be so repulsive," she yells.

"Wait." Cass sits up, suddenly awake and ready to jump into the conversation. I giggle. "What did he say?" she asks, her voice still coated in sleep.

I don't answer.

"Lennon!" she shouts, more awake now. "Text me what he said if you're too afraid to say it. I need to know why we are so repulsed by Finn!"

Appearing from around the corner, Lennon's lips pull up as her eyes sparkle with mischief. "Oh," she says, and by the tone of her voice, I know exactly where she's going. "I'm not afraid to say it. Griffin, the gentleman that he is, told Ellie they should–"

I cut her off with a pillow hurled from the couch.

"Fuck you!" she shouts, but there's no malice to be found.

Lennon plants herself on the couch, a solid foot further away from me than she was before. "I'll just text it to you," she mutters.

Thirty-Seven

Griffin

Nothing makes you more irritated at humanity than trying to deboard a plane. I'm convinced that if you can get from the airplane to baggage claim without hoping that at least one person sleeps with a hot and incredibly uncomfortable pillow, then you've been created using AI.

There is no other explanation.

As the woman in the aisle shuffles through her purse, looking for who the fuck knows, I stare at her hoping that my blinking communicates my displeasure without being an asshole.

When the woman pulls out an inhaler, and takes a dose, I regret everything I thought in the moments leading up to this realization.

She finally gets moving, and I'm free to grab my bag from the overhead bin and make my way down the tiny space between the seats.

I dig my phone out of my pocket as soon as I'm officially off the plane, stepping to the side because I like my pillows to be nice and cool when I sleep. Flipping airplane mode off, I get texts from both Lennon and Ellie, and one from Noah, too.

Ellie: *We're waiting at baggage claim.*

Lennon: *I plan on filming you two and posting it on the internet. Please pretend you're in the military, and you've been gone for months. I was thinking about writing a book, and a viral video will really help with any future sales.*

I snort a laugh, flicking to the message from Noah.

Noah: *Do you have Lennon's number?*

My brow furrows, and I type out a quick response.

Me: *Why?*

Three dots appear in the bubble at the bottom of the screen, but I don't bother waiting for his answer. I'll get to it later. Besides,

Lennon will be at baggage claim, anyway, and I need to make sure she actually *wants* Noah to have her number.

I like my dick firmly attached to my body, and based on their scuffle at the art show, the odds of her wanting him to have her number are slim to absolutely fucking not.

Walking up the ramp, I listen to the slide of my suitcase, moving my jaw in an effort to get my ears to pop.

Once they do, the murmurs become less muffled, and I quicken my pace toward the baggage claim.

The walk seems to stretch on forever.

When I finally move down the escalator, I'm shocked to find that I have what feels like another mile to go.

My phone buzzes in my pocket, and I pull it out.

Lennon: *Hurry up or we're leaving you here.*

I snort again, quickening my pace.

When she finally comes into view, my smile splits so wide I'm sure I've injured every muscle in my face.

She looks good, tired, but certainly alive and well.

I don't run–if only to ruin Lennon's stupid viral video, but when I'm standing in front of her, and she whispers, "hi," I drop my bag and wrap my arms around her. Lifting Ellie off the ground and breathing her in.

"I fucking love you." My voice is low, meant only for her, but when Lennon makes a gagging noise from where she stands with her phone held out, I know that Ellie wasn't the only one who heard.

"Hurry it up, you two!" she says, and I carefully lower Ellie to the floor.

Picking up my suitcase, I tuck her beneath my arm, refusing to let her go. "For someone who was trying to make a sweet video, you sure ruined it with your complaining," I say.

Lennon chuckles. "I'll put sappy music over it. It'll be fine."

She adjusts her backpack straps and starts walking to the conveyor belt that is slowly beginning to spit out larger luggage.

"So," I say, trailing behind her. "Noah wants your number."

Lennon's head whips around. "Absolutely fucking not."

Exactly.

"She'll kill you if you give him her number," Ellis says, and I turn to plant a kiss on her temple, my arm still firmly in place around her shoulders.

"I might risk it," I say. "Out of spite."

We grab the luggage and head out to the car where we all pile in. Between Lennon's car sickness if literally anyone else drives, and my fear of the woman, I end up in the back seat, holding Ellie's hand from her position up front.

"So," I lean forward and insert myself between them.

"Put your seatbelt on," Lennon complains, turning the air conditioning to *unbelievably frigid*. Just like her soul.

I ignore her. "They offered me a more permanent position."

Ellie turns around, her eyes lighted. "What?" she says. "You're serious!"

"Dead serious."

She pulls on her seatbelt, shifting around so she can grab my face and plant a kiss on my lips. "That's such good news."

"If you don't put your seatbelt on, you really will be *dead serious*," Lennon starts. "And sit down Ellis, I can't lose you, too." Lennon swats at her, but it doesn't wipe the grin off her face.

It's an expression I'm thankful for.

After I sent Lennon and Cass over to her house, Ellie called me the following morning. Something eased in her, and I couldn't have been more thankful for it.

She'd told me she could handle it alone, but I knew better.

Family is important when life rocks the boat. It's better to have someone out at sea with you.

As for Adam, I hope I never run into that fucker–especially after what he said to Ellis.

I reach for the aux cord, snatching it directly out of Lennon's phone and causing her to curse–violently.

Plugging in my own phone, I quickly scroll through my favorites until I find a familiar song–one that Ellie may kill me for playing on the car radio.

As soon as the strum of the guitar overtakes the vehicle, Ellie's voice floats through the air, her head in her hands.

"Oh my god, Finn. Turn that garbage off!"

I smile, leaning as far forward as I can–if only to be closer to her. "Absolutely not. We made this masterpiece. Don't you want to share it with the world?"

"It's just Lennon," she says, rolling her eyes.

"Hey," Lennon's tone is sharp as her eyes flick briefly to the stolen aux cord. "I am the world."

I laugh, sitting back in my seat as the song plays through the speakers–a reminder of that first night–the one where I laid my past bare during the quiet hours before the sun's light bled over the earth.

Ellie's cheeks are stained pink when the song ends, and Lennon quickly retrieves the cord, threatening me before promptly changing the music on the radio.

The trees pass along the highway as Lennon and Ellis go on talking about some house Lennon is looking at buying. I guess she saved enough at her job as a secretary to look into it.

I don't pay much attention, drumming my fingers on my knee and losing myself in thought–thinking back to the bucket list Ellie sent me what feels like forever ago, and wondering how many more adventures we'll get to go on.

Epilogue

Ellis

Eight Months Later

The sky is clear for December, and I'm thankful that it didn't decide to snow on my birthday.

During my sixteenth birthday, a snowstorm hit Ohio, and B freaked out. She refused to let me drive myself home, and I ended up being incredibly embarrassed at an ice rink with some guy I went on exactly two dates with.

The snowstorm one being the second and final.

Finn rented a cabin with a skylight for my birthday, insisting that the planetarium last year didn't actually count as *sleeping under the stars*. He was hellbent on completing the bucket list, which at this point seems sort of stupid.

Cass and Lennon planned a huge birthday celebration for me a few days before we left. It's not like I was alone.

I shift on the uncomfortable air mattress Finn set up directly beneath the skylight. It would have been nice if we'd moved a nicer mattress here, but instead, we are on an air mattress. Apparently, Finn wanted to sleep on the floor–just not right away. In the morning, we will be on the hardwood and surrounded by half-filled plastic.

"Listen," I say, turning to face him. His hands are folded on his chest, a smug smirk permanently etched into his face. I tuck it away to save for later, because what I'm about to say will certainly remove it. It's like when you draw with a permanent marker on a whiteboard, and then use a dry-erase marker to get it off. Not so permanent, after all. "I love that we're sleeping under the stars, but this bed is really uncomfortable. Can we call it good?"

He laughs, hazel eyes sliding my direction as he gestures for me to lay my head on his chest. I oblige, settled by the steady beating of his heart. Maybe the floor wouldn't be so bad.

"We can call this one good," he says, and I thank the universe. The floor would have certainly been bad.

Finn lifts a brow. "But we still haven't finished the bucket list."

I sit up, staring down at him. "Yes we did," I insist. "Sleeping under the stars. We just counted it as done."

Finn laughs again, a dimple forming in his cheek. "Didn't you want to do something that scared you?" he asks.

"Finn," I smile at him. "I have anxiety. Everything scares me."

This time when he laughs, I can feel it rumble across the mattress that I'm pretty sure has already started to deflate.

"I was thinking about something specific," he finally says.

I roll over, looking back up at the sky with my hands folded across my stomach. "I'm not going skydiving," I tease.

"Noah would be so disappointed."

I watch an airplane blink across the sky, cutting a path through our starry night. "I heard Noah ruined Lennon's date back in March, and she still hasn't forgiven him. I'll have to call his disappointment karma."

Finn shifts, and I keep my eyes up, finding Orion's Belt and thankful that the three stars in a row are easy to spot. Aside from that constellation, I'm at a loss.

"Something else then?" he asks, his voice quieter. The shift in tone draws my attention.

I turn to look at him, noting that he's already staring at me, a strand of dark purple hair falling across his brow.

"Out with it, Finn. You already have something in mind."

He sits up on his elbow, body facing me, when something gold flashes between us. My heart instantly decides that beating is a race, and that bitch is set on winning. "Marry me?" he says.

"What?" It's the dumbest question I've ever asked.

"I'm sorry it's not an airplane in the Bahamas, Ellie, but my job at the coffee shop and our time at the animal shelter didn't allow for more."

I look down at the ring in his hand. The gold band twists delicately, like two vines woven together. The solitaire diamond winks beneath the starlight, and my chest immediately tightens.

"Is it a no?" he says.

"Yes!" My eyes flick to his as his brows pinch together.

"So, it's a no."

"It's a yes, Stuart."

I throw my arms around him, not caring that he probably can't breathe. When he kisses me back, I can't help but think that maybe hiring someone for your birthday isn't so pitiful after all. It seemed to work out in my favor.

He breaks away, his eyes warm. "I also had a thought about to-morrow," he says.

"What is it?"

"Go on another adventure with me, Ellie." His voice is low. "I never want to be strangers again."

The End

Acknowledgements

When I started this book, there were so many things I wanted from it. For starters, I wanted to show two people falling in love and dealing with life's trials in a way that was healthy. Sometimes angst is the mood, and sometimes we just want people to stop being so stupid. The second thing I wanted from this book was, quite honestly, for this book to be exactly what I wanted to read.

Griffin and Ellis were born from everything I wanted, and I can honestly say I haven't loved one of my books this much. That being said, I've still had a full support system behind me and helping me make this thing happen.

For starters, I need to thank my brother-in-law, Nathan, for working in music and providing me with detailed emails of terms and timelines that could help make Griffin's job more believable. Without you, everyone would see me for who I truly am. An idiot. (check out natron on Spotify for some of his music)

I want to thank my sister-in-law, Sarah, for listening to me talk about this book and for suggesting I talk to her husband about the music stuff. Technically, you're the reason I don't look like an idiot because you said it first.

For my alpha readers, Wednesday, Kristin, and Livy. You were the engine that kept this thing going. Your encouragement helped at every turn. When I doubted myself, you did not (Except Wednesday. You sometimes doubt me because you've seen the worst of my typos).

Thank you to Livy Hart for providing the blurb or this book. I'm starstruck everytime we talk. You're more famous than Taylor Swift. Everyone should read your books.

Kenna, you know I wouldn't be half the writer I am without you. Every step of the way, you have supported me in your talent and your friendship. I'm so glad I met you. I can't wait to see all your books lined up next to mine on my shelf.

To Florin Coffee Shop in Ohio. Thank you for supplying the caramel lattes I needed to get this done. You will see your establishment woven into these pages.

Thank you to my main support system, my family. Without you, I wouldn't be able to do any of this. For you, I am eternally grateful.

And for you, dear reader. Thank you for making my dreams come true.